Dr. Glen Carew, recently Colonel Carew from the American theater in Korea, met Jane Grant on his first day at L.A. Midtown Hospital. The war-weary veteran knew he had never felt about another woman the way he did about this blond, vivacious nurse ... and never would again.

It seemed a lifetime, but it was just a few short days later that Jane and Glen walked into a jeweler's to choose an engagement ring. That night was their memorable night of love —tender, rapturous, feverish—a night in which they pledged to be together forever, a night in which they were impossibly happy.

But the next day tragedy struck. Jane, propped up in a hospital bed, remained blissfully, unsuspectingly, happy. The glow in her eyes was matched only by the glittering diamond she wore so proudly. But at her bedside Dr. Glen Carew watched his love, his face ashen, his heart leaden with an unbearable knowledge. . . .

Other SIGNET Books
by SHANE DOUGLAS
35¢ each

AIR SURGEON	(#S2097)
ASSISTANT SURGEON	(#S2166)
DOCTOR AT FAULT	(#S2190)
THE DOCTOR'S PLEDGE	(#S2242)
EMERGENCY SURGEON	(#S2238)
THE MERCY HEROES	(#S2078)
SKY DOCTOR	(#S2139)
SURGEON ON CALL	(#S2227)

TO OUR READERS: If your dealer does not have the SIGNET and MENTOR books you want, you may order them by mail, enclosing the list price plus 5¢ a copy to cover mailing. If you would like our free catalog, please request it by postcard. The New American Library of World Literature, Inc., P. O. Box 2310, Grand Central Station, New York 17, New York.

The Doctor's Past

by *Shane Douglas*

A SIGNET BOOK
PUBLISHED BY
THE NEW AMERICAN LIBRARY

© Copyright, 1962, by Horwitz Publications Inc. Pty. Ltd., Sydney, Australia. Reproduction in part or in whole in any language expressly forbidden in any part of the world without the written consent of Horwitz Publications Inc. Pty. Ltd.

All rights reserved

FIRST PRINTING, JUNE, 1963

SIGNET TRADEMARK REG. U.S. PAT. OFF. AND FOREIGN COUNTRIES
REGISTERED TRADEMARK—MARCA REGISTRADA
HECHO EN CHICAGO, U.S.A.

SIGNET BOOKS are published by
The New American Library of World Literature, Inc.
501 Madison Avenue, New York 22, New York

PRINTED IN THE UNITED STATES OF AMERICA

Prologue

The air hostess smiled at the last group of passengers leaving the plane. Blond, smartly uniformed, chosen for her personality and efficiency, she studied her passengers as they moved toward the exit and formed her own conclusions about each. It was a game she played with herself on each flight. The couple she had just spoken to were honeymooners, she decided, and watched a trifle enviously as the young man took his companion's arm at the foot of the steps and they walked away, smiling, their heads close together.

She knew from the passenger list that the fashionably dressed woman following them was going to Toluca Lake in North Hollywood. A dress designer, the woman wore dark sunglasses that swept up at the corners like the wings of a butterfly. The glasses made her look mysterious, exotic, like a film star traveling ostentatiously incognito.

The man crowding her heels was a realtor who worked out of one of the ornate realty offices along Sunset Boulevard. He traveled with the airlines a lot, and knew the hostesses by name. He had been attentive to the dress designer on the flight, but now his business worries were coming back. As he saw the familiar city of Los Angeles beyond the airport, time acquired the role of urgency for him again.

Yes, to an observant hostess, it was easy to form opinions about people and their motives. The air-traveling public mostly reverted to type, relaxed by the comfort, the inactivity of the traveling hours. But there were exceptions, of course. Those who withdrew, who seemed satisfied with their company, their own thoughts.

Like the last passenger—a tall man who walked slowly toward her now.

He looked like an outdoor man with those fine sun-wrinkles at the corners of his eyes, that trick of coming back to you slowly as though from a far distance when you spoke to him. He could have been an airline pilot from his obvious familiarity with planes. Or a flying rancher with that sun tan, used to tooling his own plane around some sprawling range.

Only the particulars she had of him denied that. This well-built, handsome man with the mark of character stamped on his strong face was a doctor. She glanced automatically at her list as he approached, although she remembered exactly who he was and where he had joined the flight.

Dr. Glen Carew of Calco County Hospital had joined the flight at Calco, Nevada.

He didn't look like a doctor at all, the hostess thought to herself as she smiled up at him. But he *was* attractive with sun-bleached, blond hair and one lighter colored lock straying a little across the broad, intelligent forehead. It was a strongly masculine face. His eyes were dark brown, and with those dark black brows and eyelashes, he looked almost Spanish.

"Dr. Carew? From Calco, isn't it?" She spoke crisply, but pleasantly.

"That's right." Eyes that hadn't seemed to see her before, except when she spoke, considered her.

"I hope you found everything to your satisfaction on the flight, Doctor?"

"Sure did," he said, smiling.

She followed him down the steps and together they walked the short distance to the terminal doorway.

"Guess you're mighty glad another flight's over?" he asked.

She turned a pert, oval face toward him. "It's always swell to get home again, Doctor. Even if home's only an apartment you share with another girl."

He nodded. "Sure. But flying's great fun. I like it."

"You do a lot?"

"Where I come from, we have a flying ambulance serv-

THE DOCTOR'S PAST

ice. I'm often called out. I also have a small plane of my own. Flying is a relief from hospital work."

"I can understand that," she said sympathetically. "Are you going to practice in L.A., Doctor?"

He shook his head. "No, this is just a vacation." His smile was a little twisted suddenly. He added, "I call it walking in old footprints."

"Then you've lived here before?"

"And practiced here. At L.A. Midtown Hospital."

"Golly, I left an appendix there once." She laughed. "Well, have fun on your vacation, Doctor!" They had reached the lounge. "Maybe I'll see you on your return trip."

He barely noticed her turn away and walked through the lounge, his dark eyes clouded with sudden pain.

"Have fun?" he thought bitterly as he studied the distant shape of the city beyond the International Airport. He could see the squat bulk of Midtown Hospital low down among the ragged forest of much higher buildings. He was conscious of depression. "Hell, who is there left to have fun with, anyway? Don Fenton went East when he finished his residency. Blake died when he rode an ambulance into a truck. Died with his patient, child with a ruptured appendix. Linton? Preedy? Morganthal?" They were all gone now.

Dr. Glen Carew shook his head as he passed through the terminal. All the resident doctors would have left Los Angeles Midtown General Hospital years ago. Crop after crop of interns would have come and gone, as green, as full of know-it-all, as wet behind the ears as Jeff Wilson had been.

Even the nursing staff would have changed greatly by now. They would have married, moved on....

The pain in his dark eyes deepened as he walked from the building and glanced toward the distant hospital. Nurses married....

Yes, and nurses died!

Like Jane Grant, the girl he had wanted to marry.

"When you love someone, you just can't end it. Even if death intervenes, it goes right on...."

The words came to his mind unbidden and he remembered the words and the occasion. He had said that to another nurse, a girl who believed that she loved him. Back in Calco County, Nevada, he had said those words to lovely red-haired Kathie Forrest.

He remembered the way her eyes had widened. "Always?" she had asked despairingly. "It never ... fades?"

And seeing the hurt in her steady gray eyes, he hadn't been able to answer. Because for the first time since Jane died, he had doubted.

"I don't know any more," he thought, frowning in confusion. "Not any more. The years pass and memories seem to lose strength. Perspective wavers, the picture becomes vague. Perhaps when someone you love dies, the love renews itself in someone else. ..."

That was why he was here, already knowing remembered pain—already seeing Jane again clearly in his mind as he looked at the outline of the hospital on the horizon.

"I must *know*," he thought. "I must be sure."

He owed that to the memory of Jane. He owed it to Kathie Forrest—gentle Kathie, demanding nothing. And in a way, he supposed, he owed it to himself.

He became aware that a cab had pulled in at the curb beside him, with the driver looking at him inquiringly from beneath a peaked cap. He nodded. The driver opened the door and grinned at him cheerfully.

"Any luggage, sir?"

"It's been sent on. Take me to the Alexandria, Fifth and Spring, till I check in."

"Fifth and Spring it is."

Dr. Glen Carew settled back in the seat. "After that I want you to take me to the Midtown Bar and Grill. It's a little place on Kendall, just behind the hospital."

"I know it," the driver said cheerfully. He closed the door and the cab pulled away from the curb. "Mostly hospital folk go there. Nurses and young doctors from Midtown. I guess *they* don't have time to pick and choose. But if you're interested in eating well—?"

"I'm not." Glen Carew was in no mood for a guided tour. "Just take me to the Midtown Bar as soon as I check in."

The Midtown Bar. That was where it had all started. After the war to end all wars, after the beginning of the aftermath that was Korea.

He'd felt strange in his new civilian clothes that fall in '56 as he prepared to step back into the life of a city hospital. Uncertain. Not yet accustomed to being called anything but Colonel Carew. ...

Chapter One

Dr. Stanley Prentice was slim, straight-backed, with an easy smile that denied the often-sharp expression in his brown eyes. His smooth, reddish-brown hair glinted in the light above the office table as he walked around the desk to face Dr. Glen Carew. For the chief of the surgical service at a hospital as large and important as Midtown General, Prentice looked young.

The easy smile disclosed white teeth as the door opened and a short, dark-haired, brown-eyed man in the white coat of a resident entered. The newcomer looked from Prentice to Carew inquiringly, and his eyes lingered, studying Carew. He had to look up to do that, because he stood only five feet eight to Carew's six one.

Prentice introduced them. "Don, this is Dr. Glen Carew, our new resident for the surgical service. Carew, meet Don Fenton. Don will show you your quarters in the residence. As he's off duty tonight, he might even show you around the hospital. How about it, Don?"

"Glad to!" Fenton said. "Glen Carew?" His eyes were puzzled as he shook hands, then recognition dawned suddenly. "Hell's bells! Major Carew! Tokyo—in fifty-one!" He was laughing suddenly. "Don't you remember me?"

Smiling, Carew looked almost boyish. "Of course! It was Captain Fenton then, wasn't it? You'd been transferred from Korea?"

"And hated it," Fenton nodded. "If I remember right, you weren't sold on being transferred back to Japan either. They'd put you in charge of the burn wards. We consoled one another with sukiyaki and sake. Ugh!"

"That was a while back," Carew said. "And since we only met once, you must have had the father of all hangovers to remember it!"

"I did," Fenton admitted ruefully. "What a night! But I heard of you often enough afterward. Reconstructive surgery, burns. . . ." He was looking at Carew curiously. "That's why I didn't associate you with the vacant residency here. Not even when I heard it had gone to a Dr. Carew. Last I heard, you were running an army hospital somewhere."

"Colonel Carew only left the armed services a month ago, Doctor," Prentice intervened mildly. "Their loss is our gain. He'll be doing general surgery here for the term of his residency. We'll let him settle in tomorrow, do some observing maybe. After that, I think we can keep him busy here."

"Department of understatement," Fenton said, grinning. "And it was Colonel, not Major, eh?"

"They kept me with the patients I'd treated from Korea. And of course there were others coming in, even in peacetime," Carew said. He frowned. "Accidents . . . burns, mutilating injuries, that sort of thing. Reconstructive surgery. It's . . . slow. Some Korean veterans only had the final phase of surgery a month before I left." He paused. "I stayed until the last of my patients was discharged."

Fenton nodded. That tied in with what he remembered of Glen Carew. But a full colonel's pay was way ahead of that of a resident at Midtown. And being a colonel carried prestige. You couldn't go much higher than that in the medical service of the armed forces. Carew would have been better off there than even Prentice was here as head of the surgical service. So why leave it? Fenton was puzzled.

"Fifty-six now and the last of your boys just discharged, eh? Well, I guess you had to run out of patients sooner or later."

"I didn't run out of patients," Carew answered thoughtfully. "They were still coming. Even in training, they turn over trucks. Get crushed. Burned. Accidentally shot. Injured in explosions. There's plenty of work back there all right, only . . ."

"Only what?"

"The job I started on a South Pacific island in forty-five ended when the last Korean veteran walked out of the hospital. I'd... had enough. I'm through. Plastic surgery's not my line. I want to specialize in general surgery." His tone held a faint trace of bitterness. "I got sidetracked by war, but that's over. It isn't Colonel Carew any more. It's Dr. Carew. The job's finished. Now I can do the things I want. All of them!"

Fenton glanced at Dr. Prentice, who was frowning now as he listened. The surgical chief shuffled the pile of paperwork on his desk, indicating to Fenton at least that the interview was ended.

"I'll show you your new home, Doctor," Fenton said pleasantly. "You get a two-room suite. Not the Roosevelt—but a long way ahead of Korea and other places you've known. After that, what say we have a drink at the Midtown Bar and meet some of the other guys? The Midtown's our off-duty meeting place." His glance at Dr. Prentice was slightly malicious. "It serves all ranks beneath that of chief of service. They can afford something a little better."

Carew looked at his service chief uncertainly, his brown eyes noting Prentice's frown. "Is there anything else, Dr. Prentice?" he asked quietly.

"No."

"Then I'll say good night."

"I'll expect to see you in the morning at ten, Dr. Carew." Prentice's tone held authority. "Rounds. You'll see some of your future patients on the surgical floor. Good night."

Fenton was holding the door open when Dr. Prentice added sharply, "Oh, Carew—there is one thing."

"Yes?"

"If you intend to make a habit of going to the Midtown, wear a white coat. Back of the hospital it's a tough neighborhood. They respect us here—to an extent. Never know when they might need us to patch them up. So a white coat's a form of insurance." He nodded. "That's all."

"Thanks," Carew said with a quiet chuckle. "However, I was reared in a tough neighborhood, Doctor."

As Prentice watched the door close, the phone burred on his desk. He reached for it instinctively. "Dr. Prentice."

"Well, Stanley—what d'you think of him?" a voice boomed. The loud, familiar tones belonged to Dr. Cape, Midtown's medical superintendent.

"Carew?" Prentice asked mildly.

"Who the hell else would I be asking about? Harry Truman? Of course, Colonel Carew! The guy still there?"

"He's just left."

"Well?"

"He has . . . excellent qualifications," Prentice parried.

"Dammit, man, I know all about his qualifications! I've read about him, heard about him, know what the Army thinks. It's all good. Maybe too darned good to be true! What the hell's he doing here as a resident? The guy's got an international reputation for plastic surgery, the rehabilitation of the burned and mutilated. What's he want from us?"

"To go back to where he started," Prentice said flatly. "He wants to practice general surgery."

The booming voice made an angry sound. "I could've read you that sentence from his letter of application! What's your *opinion* of him, Stanley? Know what everyone else has to say, now I want to hear your slant."

"Surely, Doctor, after speaking to the man for five minutes, you don't want me to give you his character analysis?"

There was another indignant snort. "Quit stalling, Stanley! I want to know what you think of this Carew now that you've met him face to face."

Prentice sighed. "All right. If you really want to know. I think he has the potential to be the best surgeon you've ever had in the service—"

"Good!"

"—Or else . . ."

"What?" Dr. Cape snapped.

"Or else," Prentice finished calmly, "you're going to be damned sorry you ever recommended his application. Carew's a guy who, to use his own words, got sidetracked by war. He got caught up in a whirlwind that's only just dropped him. Maybe he's still a little dazed by the drop. But he's lost a large chunk of his life by frustration. And he feels life owes him plenty for that. He wanted to practice general surgery and he wasn't able to do it. He was one square peg that got punched into a round hole so deep it couldn't see anything but the walls that confined it. Men burned and scarred, made neurotic by multilating injuries. And if Carew's human, the way I look at it, he could be going to do all the little things he's missed in those years. *All* the things."

He listened to a worried silence.

"Huh!" Dr. Cape boomed disgustedly. "A goddam lot of help you turned out to be!"

The phone banged down.

Dr. Stanley Prentice shook a cigarette from the pack on his desk and lit it. From where he sat he could look out the window to the front of the residence building across the parking area. Two figures were coming down the steps, one tall and slightly stooping as he listened to what his shorter companion was saying.

They certainly hadn't taken long. The two residents could have barely had time to dump Carew's bags and come out again. Now they were going back along the drive toward the rear entrance to the hospital and the Midtown Bar and Grill.

He had been meaning to speak to Fenton about that. Fenton was a good surgeon, but he constantly built up tensions that only the anesthesia of the Midtown Bar seemed able to relieve. Some veterans were like that. Was Carew?

Prentice got up abruptly and went over to draw the blind, shutting himself in with a pile of case histories. Drawing the blind, he could see them only as vague shadows already becoming lost among the shrubs that lined the drive. . . .

Fenton was saying, "Stanley's not too bad, really, Glen. Bit of a bluenose, but all for the service. And he's a damned good surgeon in his own right. Specialized in neurosurgery. He's well worth watching in the O.R."

"He didn't sound enthusiastic about this place you're taking me to."

"He isn't. But what the hell? We're all big boys and what we do when we're off call doesn't concern our surgical service chief—not unless what we do starts to interfere with our work."

"Sounds reasonable enough, Don."

"It is! Wait till you're on call in the Emergency Room one Saturday night. You'll think you're back in Korea. Never a moment—goddammit! You have to get away from *that* sometimes."

Carew chuckled. "It's why I'm here."

"No flies, on you, pal, I can see," Fenton said approvingly. "So we'll have us a good time." His face lost its cheerful grin suddenly. "Seriously though, Glen, aside from being stuffy about the guys going to the Midtown, Stanley's okay.

Has a sense of loyalty to the residents in his service and even to the interns. Nobody else allowed to beat his dogs! And to tell the truth—he isn't hard to work with."

"I liked him."

"Uh-huh. Well, don't get to like him too early. Takes quite a while to get to know Dr. Stanley Prentice. Most of the other doctors in the surgical service are run-of-the-mill. You'll meet two of them here tonight—Blake and Morganthal. Blake you won't like, because Blake won't like you. He's been senior resident for a year since Alsop went to San Francisco. Now you come along, and—"

Carew frowned. "All I want to do here is practice general surgery."

"Maybe. But with your qualifications, Blake is as good as out. Anyway, Paul Blake's a stinker. But you'll find that out for yourself soon enough, so forget what I said. Morganthal is okay. Nothing brilliant, but steady. A good guy to have around. The other guys in the service are on call tonight. Tom Linton and Keith Preedy. You'll meet them tomorrow. Then there are the interns. Wilson is the most likely of a mediocre lot. He *could* make a surgeon, if he wasn't so damned know-it-all cocky. Got to keep pushing his nose in it to bear him—maybe he'll improve. The unexpected often happens with interns." A wicked gleam came into Don Fenton's eyes. "Oh, and you'll meet the girls. Midtown Bar is the one place around here where they can come in this crummy neighborhood—if they don't make the trip from the hospital alone through the back-alley short cut. The Midtown's okay for them."

"The nurses?"

"Yeah. And a few other assorted dames. We also have one female intern and two female residents, one in O.B. and the other in Pathology. None of them worth shacking with, but nice girls in their own way. Maybe too nice, so that's why—you see?"

"No. But I'm guessing."

"The nurses are another story," Fenton said, a broad grin on his rather swarthy face. He looked up and swore. "Hell, it's starting to rain again! Sunny California, my foot!"

"It's hot," Carew said.

"Yeah. It gets hotter when it rains. And thirstier. I've taken you the long way around tonight. You can cut through the alleys, but like I said—that's not always safe. A lot of

THE DOCTOR'S PAST

unpleasant things can happen to a guy on his own in some of those streets. But there's the Midtown ahead. See the lights. Come on, we'll run for it."

He ran. Solidly. His shoes thumping on a pavement already starting to glisten wetly. Here there seemed mostly apartment houses with steps leading up to concrete floored porches enclosed by ornamental spiked wrought-iron railings. Carew's longer legs kept up easily and they reached the entrance together as a man holding a girl's arm ran in from the other direction.

"Move over, bud," the man panted. "Let the lady in."

Drawing aside, Carew glimpsed a girl's oval face, dark eyes. White teeth glistened in the light as she laughed and ran up the steps.

Fenton said, "Hi, Blake! Maybe I should tell her about you, if she's a lady. Where did you find her?"

"She's new at Midtown. Found her circulating when I took out some gall stones. Who's this?"

He was a big man, almost as tall as Carew, but heavier. Rain shone on his dark hair beneath the lights. A neon sign flashing above them etched the words Midtown Bar and Grill in red letters that made his heavy face look flushed and angry.

"Sorry," Fenton said. "Meet the new addition to our surgical service—Glen Carew. Glen, this is Paul Blake."

"So you're Carew?" His quick handshake was perfunctory. "Do we have to call you Colonel, or do you leave that cabbage behind in the army?"

"My friends call me Glen."

Blake nodded noncommittally. "We're getting wet. Let's get the hell inside." He shook his head, scattering raindrops, and ran up the steps to join the girl waiting at the top. Almost as he reached her, he was turning her away from them toward the open doors of the Midtown Bar. Turning, she looked back at them curiously and her eyes met Carew's briefly.

The lights above the door shone on blond hair that had something of the glint of gold in it. It reminded Glen Carew of wheat straw that he had once seen freshly cut on an Australian hillside after Korea. The wheat stalks had seemed to hold the sun as her hair now held the light.

Her eyes were hazel. Honest eyes, large, intelligent. He

could not be sure whether they were predominantly gray, or brown. But he did know that she was lovely.

"Don't rush me, Doctor," she protested laughingly. "Who are your friends?"

But Blake was already guiding her away from them. Rapidly. Without looking back.

"A stinker," Fenton muttered after the retreating figure of Blake. "Like I said, Glen. Not even an introduction. Come on. There are a couple of girls I know over there with Morganthal." He gestured toward the other end of the room. "Morganthal is the big ox at the corner table. Looks like a weight lifter and handles a scalpel about the same way. But at least he's sociable. And we can easily find another girl."

He followed Fenton among tables that were pulled together as customers formed groups. But his eyes followed Dr. Paul Blake and the girl with him. Blake was drawing out a chair for her at a table that stood apart, a table for two. Blake quite evidently had no intention of sharing her company with anyone.

Moving in to the table, she looked back toward Carew again curiously and said something to Blake. He looked down the room and frowned. Her long thighs and firm breasts sprang into prominence briefly as she adjusted her skirt before she sat down and Blake's broad back barred further vision.

Morganthal reared up from behind his table to shake hands with Carew. Heavily built, he had a grip like a vice, but his face was strong, his smile pleasant.

"Mind if I call you Glen? It's always informal in here. Glen, this is Sue. And the blonde with the bedroom eyes is Diane."

They were both pretty girls, Carew saw. One dark, the other fair. They smiled at him, their eyes speculative.

Fenton said, "We're going to need another girl to make it a nice friendly gathering. How about it, Sue?"

The dark girl looked around. "I'll find someone."

Morganthal said, "Who's the blonde with Blake?"

Fenton grunted. "You couldn't get her away. He's got her chained."

"Want to bet?" Sue's eyes sparkled at Don. "She rooms next to me in the residence and she's new. She needs friends. You always do when you come to a new job in a strange

THE DOCTOR'S PAST

hospital. I'll bet you a dollar I can persuade ~ to come with us another time, though maybe not tonight

"Taken!" Fenton said. "If it's only to give the jerk she's with a jolt. I'll pay out cheerfully on that one, S. Shake!"

They shook hands solemnly across the table.

Morganthal grinned. "She's sure got just about everything, anyway. What's her name?"

"Grant. Jane Grant," the dark girl said. "And curb your polygamous instincts, Doctor. You're out with me."

Carew looked down the long room, hazed with cigarette smoke. It was dim and narrow, barely wide enough for its crowded tables. But he could see the girl down there clearly, and as he watched she looked up and caught him staring at her. He turned away, embarrassed.

"Jane," he thought. "Jane Grant. So that's your name...."

And suddenly it was as though he knew the girl with the blonde hair intimately. As though along the length of the room, through the sound of voices, the stir of movement, the rising cigarette smoke, somehow, a bond had formed between them.

"And now," Fenton said cheerfully, "while the lovely Sue ponders the question of another girl to make our night complete—let's all have a goddam drink...."

And that was the beginning.

Chapter Two

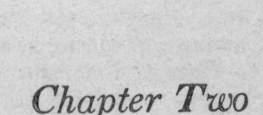

"This is Mrs. Durban, Doctor," Prentice said in a calm, cheerful voice. "How are you this morning, Mrs. Durban?"

The woman's answer came in little more than a whisper. "Mostly I don't *feel* anything to bother me, Doctor." She wet her lips with the tip of a red tongue, a young, rather attractive woman with red hair and frightened blue eyes as she studied the group of doctors and the following train of student nurses in charge of a floor nurse, who kept them at a respectful distance.

Prentice nodded. "Few people feel anything that really troubles them for quite a while. Miss Fuller, bring the nurses in closer. I want them to hear. That's better. No pain, Mrs. Durban?"

"Well, there's soreness now...."

"And a lump?"

"Yes." Her voice was husky. "I first noticed it about a month ago."

Prentice turned slightly toward the doctors. "Mrs. Durban is an intelligent young woman. That's why she's here." He nodded as the attending nurse helped the patient to remove her nightgown. The woman lay down again. She was still young. Barely thirty, Carew decided as he studied her, frowning slightly in concentration from where he stood beside a rather bored-looking Blake. She had small, rounded breasts with the areolas slightly darker in color than nip-

THE DOCTOR'S PAST

ples that had firmed with the colder air of the ward and her embarrassment.

She looked away from them, blushing as Prentice touched her left breast.

"Mrs. Durban has a lump here," Prentice said. "And a little soreness. She has a tumor that we believe is malignant. Tomorrow morning at ten-thirty, she will be prepared for a radical mastectomy. Fortunately for Mrs. Durban, she consulted her own doctor, and he decided to send her to us for tests. She consulted her doctor because her sister had the same condition four years ago. A lump, soreness, a vague feeling of something wrong there. Her sister didn't think a great deal about it until the lump started to spread and the pain became a lot worse than it is in Mrs. Durban's case. Eventually it forced her to seek medical help. We operated on her here." He faced the patient again. "How is your sister these days, Mrs. Durban?"

"Fine, Doctor," the woman answered without looking at him. "No trouble. Nothing."

"She was lucky," Prentice said. "But Mrs. Durban isn't going to *need* the same luck, because she came to us earlier. In Mrs. Durban's case the prognosis is much better. She will have the same operation but we aren't going to have the same worry about her."

The woman clenched her hands tightly. "Doctor, I had to know . . ." she breathed. "And I knew that if I . . . had it —the sooner something was done the better."

"Which was a good, intelligent decision," Prentice said, smiling at her. "Any questions?"

"Is an accurate clinical diagnosis of carcinoma of the breast possible at this stage, Dr. Prentice?"

Carew turned slightly to seek out the speaker among the group of interns. The youth was tall and thin, with sandy hair and brown eyes that had a wide, inquiring stare as he waited.

"Ah," Prentice said, looking at him. "*Doctor* Wilson! It is possible to be correct in the purely clinical diagnosis of carcinoma of the breast in approximately ninety-five percent of cases. That is more than sufficient reason for surgery in all cases. Move closer, Dr. Wilson. Put your hand here. Come on, Doctor, Mrs. Durban won't bite you!"

Wilson's brown eyes looked his embarrassment, but he moved in slowly.

"Press there," Prentice ordered. "Tell me what you feel."

Wilson palpated the smooth skin gently. The woman winced, her eyes averted.

"Harder!"

"Yes, sir. . . ."

"Well?"

"There's a lump—tenderness—" Wilson muttered uneasily.

"Now the other breast. . . . Harder."

"I can feel nothing here," Wilson said, looking up. He withdrew his fingers quickly, as though the smooth skin he had pressed was hot. At the back of the group one of the student nurses giggled. Wilson blushed, the freckles across his rather snub nose vanishing in a flood of red.

"What do you know about mastitis, *Doctor* Wilson?" Prentice asked. "Would you say that the patient *might* have chronic cystic mastitis?"

"No, I wouldn't," Wilson said angrily. "If she did, I'd expect to find a number of small, rather vague lumps in both breasts. There is only one. In the left breast. It's clearly outlined. But couldn't that mean it's still benign? Perhaps encapsulated, with no chance for metastasis?"

He was staring at the circle of amused faces around him—angry, on the defensive. Watching, Carew felt sorry for the intern and he looked away, frowning. He was beginning to dislike the slim, rather cynical Prentice.

"It means that the condition you can feel is not chronic cystic mastitis?" Prentice asked coldly.

"Of course, but—"

"If there were other lumps, Dr. Wilson," Prentice interrupted, "if our diagnosis was chronic cystic mastitis, we would not operate. That's the exception in modern surgery of the breast. It's the only lump we don't remove. But all others—*all have to come out!* Is that understood?"

"Yes," Wilson muttered, red-faced. "Yes, of course. I only thought—"

"You thought? What did you think, Doctor?"

"Well, you said radical mastectomy—I mean, all the breast. . . . You intend to remove all the breast—"

Prentice smiled at his patient. "Dr. Wilson is disturbed, Mrs. Durban. In your interest, of course." He was speaking to the patient as well as the intern now. "We need to be not ninety-five percent correct, but one hundred percent sure that it is malignant and a breast carcinoma before we perform a radical mastectomy. Tomorrow morning, you will go to the operating room prepared for that—as we will be. That's a safeguard for the patient. But we'll be hoping that what you really have is just a benign tumor. Encapsulated, as Dr. Wilson just suggested. Quite incapable of any spread. And if it is we will quite happily take it away and leave only a small scar on the breast. We will be one hundred percent sure of what it is then, because we will have seen it and we will have had it examined microscopically down in Pathology. If it's established carcinoma, that will be obvious quickly. But if there's any doubt, then you will come back to your room with the wound closed until Pathology carries out further tests. Until we are one hundred percent sure of exactly what it is. Now, are you satisfied, Dr. Wilson?"

Wilson nodded. "Yes, Doctor. I just thought—"

"And to make sure that Mrs. Durban's interests are well looked after, Wilson," Prentice said mildly, "*you* can be in the O.R. tomorrow morning. You've met Mrs. Durban's surgeon—Dr. Carew. Report to Dr. Carew at ten A.M. And Wilson..."

"Yes, Doctor?"

"Try not to get in Dr. Carew's way, or ask him foolish questions at the wrong moment."

Beside Carew, Fenton chuckled. Some of the interns and residents were also laughing as Wilson backed away, red-faced. Prentice seemed to have forgotten him now as he spoke to the duty nurse.

"I want the patient prepared for a radical mastectomy this evening, Nurse. Dr. Carew will advise the preoperative sedation later in the day. That's all, Mrs. Durban. Thank you for being so cooperative. Now, let's see what we have in the male wards...."

His entourage turned, moving to let him through, following in a low-voiced train. Carew found himself walking beside Fenton again.

"That's the first I knew I was scheduled for a radical mastectomy!" Carew said, frowning.

Fenton grinned. "Stanley's the complete autocrat. He makes the decisions around here. His saving grace is the fact that he does it as naturally as he breathes, and that he's usually right." He lowered his voice. "A lot of people think he should be running this hospital, not just the surgical service. Dr. Cape leans heavily upon Stanley's shoulder every chance he gets. He piles work feet deep onto him. But Stanley takes it all and apparently doesn't even notice that he's being imposed upon. I don't believe it's ever occurred to him that he might as well have Cape's position and Cape's salary as do his work for him."

"I wouldn't think much gets past him," Carew murmured.

"That does," Fenton said confidently. "The last time Cape's job came up for consideration, there was a real effort to get Prentice to try for it. He's got plenty of friends in high places. He would have taken it right out from under Cape's nose. Know what he said to his supporters?"

Carew shrugged. "You're telling the story."

"Said they *had* to be joking because he knew they were all loyal to the hospital and Cape. But as a joke, he thought it was in rather bad taste. He had a long way to go before he could hope to step into the shoes of as big a man as Dr. Cape. So why flatter him, when he was just a surgeon really, and doing the only job he knew how to do well."

"Doesn't Dr. Cape ever operate, or advise on treatment?"

"He advises all right," Fenton snorted. "Cape's the best goddam adviser you ever listened to. But he hasn't had a scalpel in his hand in a decade, or treated a patient. If you ever find yourself agreeing with Dr. Cape—go look up the textbooks. You're wrong."

"Well, there's more to the administration of a hospital than the mechanics of medicine," Carew said ruefully. "I learned that. That's why I'm here. I'd rather operate."

"And you will," Fenton said. "Prentice will see to that, starting with the radical mastectomy—if he doesn't decide offhand that you should even be doing something this afternoon. Listen, there goes Wilson sticking out his neck again. Move in closer. It's always worth listening when Wilson asks questions."

"Isn't it always desirable to dissect the eighth rib in a midthoracic esophagus resection for carcinoma, sir?" the lanky intern asked.

"Ah," Prentice said, looking at him. "*Doctor* Wilson again; no, it isn't always either desirable or necessary to remove the eighth rib. Hasn't it occurred to you, Wilson, that if the fifth, sixth, and seventh ribs are divided near the angle posteriorly,

THE DOCTOR'S PAST

adequate exposure can be obtained? Move in here beside me and I'll try to explain...."

"If you never ask questions, how do you learn?" Carew murmured as they moved in closer.

"But not all the time," Fenton said. "Surely not all the time. And not smirking, as though you have the answer. Wait till you get him on ward duties with you. He'll drive you nuts, unless, like Prentice and the rest of us, you rub his nose in it a little."

"You said there was hope for him as a surgeon," Carew said, only half listening to Dr. Prentice's biting sarcasms driving Wilson back in among the other interns.

"Sometimes I doubt it," Fenton sighed.

When the rounds had ended, Carew sipped hot coffee in Prentice's small office.

He said quietly, as Fenton finished and got up, closing the office door behind him on the way out, "You mentioned that I was doing a mastectomy on Mrs. Durban, Doctor?"

Prentice nodded, his penetrating eyes holding those of the younger man. "That's right. Unless of course, you'd rather take something else? There's a rectum excision. A carcinoma. I had intended to take that myself."

"I don't have any preference," Carew said. "I'll take them as they come. I want to practice general surgery. That part of it is okay. I thought it unusual though, that you should tell me indirectly in the manner you did. I'm not an intern."

"Like Wilson, you mean?" Prentice raised an eyebrow. "Did I give you the impression that I thought you were like Wilson? I hadn't scheduled any operation for you, Dr. Carew. Not until we saw Mrs. Durban on rounds. In the army, you practiced reconstructive surgery, didn't you?"

"Yes, I did." Carew frowned. "I told you I came here to get away from that."

Prentice nodded. "You were, as I remember it, mainly concerned with traumatic lesions. Burns... wounds.... You'll get many of them here, Carew. They're a part of the responsibility of general surgery. And because you're the best man for that job, you'll get them. They come through the Emergency Room every day of the week and double on weekends. I remembered that when I was examining Mrs. Durban. I also remembered that you want broader experience in general surgery. I decided a mastectomy would be as good a start as any for you here. It's as simple as that."

"I see." Carew was staring at his service chief, fighting hard to control the anger that he could feel stirring inside him.

"Have you performed a mastectomy?" Prentice demanded.

"The patients I've been attending were a little different," Carew reminded him. "Anatomically. I've assisted, of course. As an intern."

Prentice nodded, unsmiling. "And that was quite a long while ago. If I were you, I'd do some research on it tonight. Most surgeons these days use the Halsted operation. I'd study that. And I'd also take over the preoperative preparation of my patient."

"Which is another way of suggesting I should stay in the residence tonight?" Carew's tone was curt.

Prentice nodded. "I hardly think you'll find time to visit the Midtown Bar with Fenton, or whoever happens to be available. But that's entirely up to you. I'm not placing you on call nights until you settle in. Fenton will assist you in the morning."

"*And* Dr. Wilson, I think you said."

Prentice smiled. "I did tell Wilson to scrub in, didn't I? Well, he'll do that. Let him tie off a bleeder or two. Give him a retractor to hold. Have him tie sutures. Each year we get a new crop of surgical interns here. And each year we get one, or if we're lucky, two, who have what we're looking for. This year it's Wilson. The world needs surgeons, Carew. It needs them very badly."

"I'll try to remember that," Carew said stiffly.

Prentice waited until Carew reached the door before he said sharply, "Dr. Carew."

"Yes?" Carew was looking back at him, his eyes expressionless.

"You'll take the mastectomy in the main operating suite. That means you'll have quite a number of observers. This is a public hospital in a big city, not a military hospital in a restricted area. So you'll have a gallery of students, interns, and the curious from this hospital who may be interested and free. Dr. Cape will probably be there. There will be a microphone over the table, but you won't have to worry about it. You won't be expected to do anything else but operate. Fenton will give a short introduction, and the case history, while he prepares the operative area."

"So—?" Carew could no longer keep the anger from his brown eyes.

Prentice nodded mildly. "That's all, Carew. Just thought you should know. Better look in on Mrs. Durban before you go to lunch. This afternoon you can either observe in the operating suites, or work with the surgeons on ward duties. Please yourself."

"Thank you," Carew said. He added bitterly beneath his breath as he closed the door of Prentice's office: "For nothing, you son of a bitch!"

"Good morning, Doctor," a girl's voice said as he walked down the passage toward the operating suites. Pleasant, girlish, it brought Carew back from the anger he felt at Dr. Stanley Prentice and his off-hand disposal of other people's time and lives.

His anger vanished as he found Sue Callaghan dimpling at him from the shelter of a small serving kitchen that served the surgical floor.

"Hello, Sue."

Last night Sue Callaghan had monopolized Carew and it had seemed to him that it was intentional on her part. She had found another girl easily enough for Fenton. It occurred to him now, as it had then, that since neither Fenton nor Morganthal had seemed to worry about that, Sue must have no romantic ties there of any permanency. Now, he found that thought rather pleasant.

"Well," she said, lowering her voice and looking past him a little anxiously. "Don't stand out there where everyone can see you, Doctor. Come in and visit."

"If it's okay?"

"Who cares if it is or isn't?—that is, if you haven't something really important you have to do."

"Hardly," he said. "I can observe in the O.R. or work in the wards. Nobody seems very interested where. You're not busy?"

"Me? I'm always busy!" she said cheerfully and almost closed the door behind him, leaving it open only a crack. Her smile impish, she came back to where coffee steamed in an urn. "Got rules about being closed in serving kitchens with handsome doctors," she said, jerking her dark head toward the door. "Not that *I'd* mind. Like some coffee?"

"I could use it," he said, smiling.

She *was* pretty all right. Beneath her cap, her dark hair had the gloss of health that went with her clear gray eyes. Slim, but with a nurse's sure movements and almost stately walk. Beneath the crisp uniform he could see the slight rise and fall of pert, thrusting breasts.

"I'll bet," she said. "I might even find something a little special for *you*. Like some chicken to go in the sandwich, if you care for chicken?" She bent, searching in the small refrigerator. "Uh-huh! It's here. I thought for a moment that Jane might have found it. She was in here getting coffee for Dr. Blake...."

"Jane?"

She straightened, her smooth face a little flushed. "Jane Grant, the blond girl with Paul Blake in the Midtown last night. Remember? The girl Don Fenton and I had a bet about?"

Carew frowned. "I remember her."

"We room next to each other," she said. "That's why I bet Don. I could lose though. Nearly daylight when she came in. Paul Blake doesn't believe in losing time when the new girl around here happens to be attractive. And Jane is that. The coffee is a bad sign, too. Paul believes in keeping them where he can see them for a while. Means he likes her, doesn't want to give her up. And he can be awfully possessive. Don't I know it!"

"Do you?" he said.

She giggled. "I was new here too, once." She brought the coffee and sandwich to where he leaned against the scrubbed shelf. "Cream, if you like it, Doctor. Or is it all right to call you Glen?"

"It's okay with me on both counts," he said, smiling.

"That's fine, Glen. Enjoy yourself last night? It's good to get away from it all sometimes, isn't it?"

"I hardly know," he said ruefully. "Never have had much chance to get away from it before."

She poured herself black coffee, and stirred it absently. "Last night was rather crowded though. I mean, there were *six* of us. I think sometimes it's better fun when there's just two. When it's ... more intimate."

He studied her interestedly. "Last night I was just get-

THE DOCTOR'S PAST

ting to know the people I'm to work with here. I tried to meet as many of them as I could. But you're right about that."

"There are other places beside the Midtown," she said tentatively. "Although most of the people here can't see anything else. I like to go to a show sometimes, don't you? And afterward maybe have a drink. A few of the girls here live out, share apartments, that sort of thing. They have fun. For the rest of us who live in the residence—well, it gets a bit grim."

"I can imagine," he said. "Why don't we do that together? See a show downtown one night?"

"I'd love it." Her smile was slightly triumphant. "I'm off duty nights all this week, Glen."

He nodded. "I start surgery tomorrow. Dr. Prentice has decided I should read up on a mastectomy tonight. But tomorrow night—? Did you have a show in mind?"

"You name it."

"We'll see what's playing," he said. "I'll pick you up outside the residence. I have a car—"

"All that, and a car too!" she said. She laughed happily. "I believe I'm going to like you a lot, Glen Carew."

"I hope so, Sue."

"Know something?"

"What?"

"Right now I do. Right now—"

Her hands reached out and caught his shoulders, and she rose on her toes to kiss him on the mouth. Her lips were full and warm, and parted against his mouth. The tip of a warm tongue touched him briefly before she withdrew. The cup rattled in its thick saucer as he put it down quickly and reached for her. But she was gone.

"Tomorrow night, Glen," she said happily. Her expression changed abruptly. She listened. "Drink your coffee, I'll have to go now!" she said in a low voice. "There's someone coming." She marshaled cups and saucers with amazing speed, picked up her tray. Opening the door, she glanced back at him, dark eyelashes drooping, making her gray eyes provocative.

"Eight o'clock outside the nurses' residence," she said quickly. "Don't be late, because I won't be. When I want something, I go right after it...."

Chapter Three

"Since the lymphatic vessels beneath the skin serve as pathways for the spread of cancer cells, Dr. Carew will remove not only the entire breast, but also the regional lymphatic glands and neighboring muscle and fascia in which metastasis may have already occurred even this early in the course of the disease...."

Carew waited, standing aside while his assistant, Dr. Don Fenton, painted the operative area, then surrounded it with sheets and green towels, and spoke toward the microphone as he worked. Glen Carew glanced up at the glass-fronted gallery that opened upon one side of the big room. The seats up there were padded comfortably and rose in tiers, a half dozen seats in each row and almost all of them filled. The observers were talking among themselves, but inside the operating room there was no sound other than Fenton's voice.

"The female breast has an abundant blood supply, mainly from branches of the internal mammary, the intercostal, and the axillary arteries. While a good blood supply is essential in healing in carcinoma of the breast, the blood supply is a factor that Dr. Carew will have to consider very seriously in the possible spread of cancer cells...."

The breast, painted scarlet with antiseptic now, rose and fell as the patient breathed. Waiting, Carew checked again, his memory recalling the operation that he had studied in-

THE DOCTOR'S PAST

tently last night, while his eyes ran again over the operating room and its contents. Behind the screen that hid the patient's face and head, the anesthesiologist was checking his dials, his fingers busy as he watched the patient's needs.

Gas anesthesia was satisfactory in breast amputation and the anesthesiologist, Dr. Bob Howarth, seemed to know his job well. He was nursing the patient along, holding her nicely in the second plane of anesthesia. He caught Carew studying him, and winked reassuringly.

"She's quite ready, Dr. Carew," he said in a low voice. He gave the readings of blood pressure, pulse, and respiration. "You shouldn't have any trouble. She's in very good shape."

Carew nodded. He wished that Fenton would stop talking like a professor so that he could get on with it. Every time he looked at the operative area he felt something close to dismay. The feeling, he knew, stemmed from the long years of Army Medical surgery. There had been only men in his wards. The skin flesh and tissue that he had cut had been male. All male....

But here was a woman's breast. Smooth, rounded, soft—bearing no outward indication of any disease at all. It seemed sacrilege.

He glanced up at the gallery again, and watched Dr. Cape sit down heavily in the front seat, with his neighbors leaning away from his bulk as he settled in.

Prentice had said that Dr. Cape would be there, but it added to his uneasiness now. He was beginning to feel that Dr. Prentice had arranged it like this to embarrass him. He frowned around the room, checking instruments. The electrocautery unit was in place, near where Jeff Wilson stood watching the transfusion. Later, Wilson would help him cauterize small vessels that the woman on the table could do without.

His eyes moved farther. The scrub nurse stood beside the mobile tray of gleaming instruments, which had been wheeled over the patient's legs. She had wide young eyes of a soft brown above her mask, and her forehead had the smoothness of youth, but she looked efficient. The older Chief Operating Room nurse was on hand this morning, personally checking on all her O.R. staff's preparations and procedures —a function she performed at frequent intervals in each of the various operating rooms.

The circulating nurse had her used-instrument receptacles organized just outside the area of glaring white light around the table. A tall, willowy girl, she had her head bent over her utensils. . . .

She looked up suddenly as though she felt his eyes upon her. Momentarily their eyes met above their masks. Carew stared. Last night he had wondered if those eyes were gray or brown, because they had seemed so dark. Now he knew that they were gray-green. Clear and challenging, they held his astonished gaze briefly before she looked down again.

Jane Grant!

"I found her circulating . . ." Blake had said. He had meant that literally. Jane Grant was a circulating nurse, the one in the O.R. team who stayed just outside the sterile area where only scrubbed and gloved personnel might work. She must be available at all times for a variety of duties—to help the anesthetist, perhaps, or to supply the scrub nurse or surgeon with anything needed unexpectedly from the Supply Room or the autoclaves.

Glen Carew found that knowledge unexpectedly pleasing. It meant that he would be seeing quite a lot of Jane Grant in here on the long schedules of surgery.

"Dr. Carew will now begin," Fenton's voice said. "Miss Grant, swing the microphone away and start the clock. Right, Dr. Carew? It's all yours now."

The surgeon drew a deep breath and held out his hand for the first instrument. A scalpel touched his palm. Weighing it, getting the feel of it between his fingers, he watched Jane Grant swing the long arm that held the microphone back against the wall.

He found it difficult to look down at the operative area. He drew his brows together, forcing concentration.

He had chosen the Orr incision instead of the Halsted as recommended by Dr. Prentice. Last night he had been able to think of sound reasons in favor of the Orr. Only now, as he poised the scalpel, with the bright light above him glinting on the fine steel blade, he could not be sure of those reasons. Had he chosen the Orr because Prentice had suggested the Halsted? Perhaps that was the reason, born of a natural stubbornness, resentment even.

But the Orr incision was *good,* he told himself firmly now. It used a triangular axillary flap of skin, and that must give a

THE DOCTOR'S PAST

good exposure of the axillary area beneath the smooth, outstretched arm.

"Axillary dissection is the most difficult part of the operation," the textbooks of last night had warned. "It should be done with extreme care so that no cancerous tissue is left attached to the nerves or vessels...."

Wasn't that in itself a sufficient reason? The axillary area was a network of nerves and vessels....

He bent, reassured, closing his mind against thoughts of Prentice—and against vague, intruding thoughts of the blond circulating nurse now watching him as curiously as the others were.

He glanced once at the transfusion. Five percent dextrose. That should be sufficient support for the unconscious woman on the table if hemostasis was carefully carried out. And he meant to be careful about hemostasis. Very careful. If there was heavy blood loss, he would have to start a whole-blood transfusion at once to combat shock.

He made the first stroke firmly and was glad that he had. A woman's skin was just as tough as a man's. He found it was surprisingly strong and resistant despite its deceptive smoothness.

The skin parted below the axilla, a steady red seepage following the blade. The lump was high. He was glad, because this first stage of the Orr incision meant that he could make the exploratory incision a part of the whole, just the way he had planned last night. The mottled surface of fascia showed beneath the skin. Blood welled quickly, and he rested while Fenton sponged the area and closed off the bleeder. He finished the transverse incision then and turned, cutting around the underside of the breast.

There was, he knew, a current controversy on the advisability of cutting through suspect tissue. If you cut through cancerous tissue to take a specimen for biopsy, the chances were that you loosed cancer cells with the spilled blood, to metastasize later. He could feel the lump plainly now with his fingers. And he meant to dissect the whole of it out, with the minimum of blood loss, with no rupture or incision of the lump itself to release a flood of cancer cells.

He worked almost silently with only an occasional word to his assistant surgeon, Fenton.

"Retract."

"Yes, Doctor."

"Hold the flap up. That's it! I'm going to take the whole tumor away...."

"Ligate...."

"Forceps...."

It cleared slowly, an irregular mass of cells almost as large as a pigeon's egg. A blue-purple mass that reminded him of the nodules of a lung cancer that he had once seen unexpectedly through a bronchoscope.

"Encapsulated?" Fenton asked in an anxious voice.

He shook his head. It was malignant all right, he was sure of that now. He was taking neighboring tissue with it, cutting painstakingly so as not to cut the mass itself. He lifted it gently with blunt-jawed forceps as it cleared. He showed it to Fenton, who swore beneath his breath.

"Miss Kline. Have this rushed to Pathology. They're expecting it."

"Miss Grant!" the Chief Operating Room nurse said sharply in response. "Miss Grant! Take this to Pathology. Hurry!"

She was holding out a receptacle to him at once. He dropped the specimen in, still held in the forceps. Their eyes met again briefly.

He said quietly, "Tell Dr. Curtis to rush it. We'll wait."

"Shall I wait for the result, Doctor, or will Dr. Curtis call the annex?" She had a soft voice, slightly husky. An exciting voice....

"I'd like you to wait, Miss Grant, and bring the result back as soon as it comes through."

"Yes, Dr. Carew."

Fenton said, "Well, what do *you* think?"

"Malignant. And you?"

"I agree," Fenton said, frowning. "The mastectomy will have to be performed. And we'll save time if we keep going."

"Curtis said before I scrubbed that he'd give us a decision fast," Carew said, frowning. "We'll complete hemostasis as far as we've gone, rather than incise deeper before we're sure. Agreed?"

Fenton nodded. He felt better about Midtown's new surgeon suddenly. Carew had appeared hesitant at first, but he was doing better now. He had plenty of confidence. Fenton managed a smile behind his mask. "You're the surgeon!"

"How is she, Dr. Howarth?" Carew asked.

"Pressure has fallen slightly, Doctor," the anesthetist said.

THE DOCTOR'S PAST

"But she's standing up to it well. Pulse and respiration are near normal."

Carew nodded. "Dr. Wilson, move the electrocautery unit in closer. We'll seal off the small vessels while we're waiting. Dr. Fenton, will you keep the operative area clear?"

Nervously Wilson wheeled the white porcelain machine closer. Carew held out his hand for the electrode.

"Cauterizing current, Doctor. Switch on. I'll work it from this end. Right?"

The switch clicked as Wilson turned it on. Carew drew out the severed end of a small bleeder and touched it with the electrode. It hissed faintly and the end of the vein turned black with a tiny plop of sound. He moved to the next as Fenton, working in rhythm, sponged and moved back. The bleeding along the line of the incision stopped slowly. Carew nodded.

"Now we'll take the larger ones. Ligature, Nurse."

His fingers slid it over a hemostat almost as it touched his palm and he was tying. He freed the hemostat.

"Another ligature, please."

"Will we go in if there's no word from Pathology?" Fenton asked in a low voice.

"Yes." But he was aware of movement suddenly and he saw Jane Grant hurrying in, her forehead flushed above her mask.

Fenton said anxiously, "Well?"

"Dr. Curtis says the result is positive, Doctor!" She spoke breathlessly. "It's a carcinoma."

Her eyes held pity as she looked down at the patient suddenly. They were expressive eyes that seemed to mirror her moods. Carew looked away.

"Scalpel, Nurse."

Now he cut more boldly and Fenton had to work more quickly to keep up as he cleared the area and clipped bleeders. Carew was deceptively fast, he was finding now. And he was starting to work surely, the earlier hesitation completely gone. Fenton cleared the area and leaned away from the table, gesturing to his forehead where sweat had beaded. Jane Grant came in with a towel to mop it away.

Carew was extending the incision to surround the breast now, incising deeper. The scalpel turned away, undercutting the skin away from the island of remaining skin about the paling areola and nipple. Fenton came in to retract the flaps of skin from the operative area, and clip them there. Carew rested briefly. He glanced at the circulating nurse and she picked up a towel quickly, her eyes questioning. He shook his head. No. He was not sweating. He felt surer now, less uncertain. It made no difference that it was a woman beneath his scalpel. She needed his help as much as any of the mutilated men he had brought back reluctantly from death in other days. And he was confident now that he could give her that help.

Fenton stepped back. He bent again. Now, the muscle. . . .

He was identifying the pectoralis major muscle, dissecting it free at its apex high under the armpit. He worked a forefinger beneath it, raising it.

"Scalpel . . ."

He cut through the big muscle high up, exposing the smaller muscle beneath and Fenton drew the big muscle back and down with a heavy hemostat as he dissected it clear with blunt finger dissection. He treated the minor muscle in the same manner, dissecting, severing, drawing it down.

Carew straightened and studied the area. Now the fat and fascia covering the axillary nerves and vessels was exposed and must be carefully dissected free from the vessels and nerves within—dissected so carefully that no remnant remained that could contain cancerous cells.

He bent again. He began the slow, meticulous dissection.

He was peeling the whole mass downward, Fenton saw. "Like a damned banana skin," he thought in relief. There should not be much trouble there. Not if Carew had the ability to do it. And he was beginning to think that Carew had.

Fenton glanced quickly up at the gallery. He had forgotten about the observers, as he was sure Carew had. But the men up there were watching tensely as that mass of tissue rolled back slowly. There were risks, of course. The vessels and nerves—! Fenton looked back anxiously.

Carew was baring the long nerves now and Fenton could see the outline of the ribs quite plainly as they bared to the deep thoracic tissues. The chest wall was exposed. Fenton could see the ribs and the long thoracic nerve. Carew was taking all the anterior fascia tissue right down to the rectus abdominis muscle.

He was ligating the branches of the main vessels, closing off those along the sternum from the internal mammary, closing other smaller vessels with electrocautery. He stepped back and his eyes met those of Fenton above his mask. Fenton smiled reassuringly as he saw anxiety mirrored there momentarily.

He said, "Ready to take it away?"

"Yes. We'll lift it off in one mass. Then we'll have another look at the area. Miss Grant!"

The circulating nurse came in with a covered bucket and held it ready. The surgeon and assistant lifted gently, holding the edges of the mass gripped between strong forceps. It cleared. They lowered it into the waiting receptacle and the circulating nurse covered it quickly, her eyes a little sick.

"Take that to Pathology too, Miss Grant," Carew said. He let his breath sigh out. "Tell Dr. Curtis we'll expect a report on the possibility of metastasis tomorrow."

"Yes, Doctor." She searched for the interest she had seen in his eyes earlier, but he looked away. Disappointed, she moved back with the receptacle as he spoke to Fenton.

"We'll ligate all bleeders now, or cauterize. I'll take the electrocautery with Dr. Wilson. . . ."

The operation moved on smoothly. Now only clean, surgically dissected tissues showed, unbroken except for the severed ends of the pectoralis muscles beneath the armpit, and below where the breast had been.

The long nerves and their branches showed against the ribs, preserved; the long thoracic nerve running down across the ribs, the shorter, thicker sub-thorac-dorsal nerve paralleling its course.

They ligated carefully, the gallery of observers forgotten in the needs of the moments before closure. There were a lot of small bleeders that must be closed. But the area cleared slowly, the steady seepage stopped as the electrocautery unit hissed and Fenton tied carefully placed ligatures about the larger vessels and closed them off.

Fenton tied the last ligature and straightened, grinning. "Ready to close, Dr. Carew."

Carew nodded. "Yes. We're ready. How is she, Dr. Howarth?"

"Pulse is weaker. Pressure falling. I'm giving her oxygen now to help respiration." He gave the readings from instruments and chart a little anxiously. "How much longer, Doctor?"

"Probably another hour. I'll start whole blood transfusion. Dr. Wilson! Whole blood. Five hundred cc.s."

He bent, studying the area within the drawn-back flaps of skin.

"Sutures now.... Dr. Fenton, we're going to anchor the flaps with sutures taken through the skin and anchored in the deep muscles or tissue of the chest wall to eliminate dead space and reduce tension on the skin margin."

Fenton leaned forward, interested. "That's new to me. But I can see its value."

"It's used in plastic surgery. Saves contracture, and possible pockets of infection. We'll place them at the apex of the axilla first."

Frowning, Fenton watched him place the first suture through the flap of skin deep in the severed end of the pectoralis muscle high up beneath the armpit. It drew that portion of flap tightly into place. The pattern of the anchoring sutures formed slowly. And Fenton saw with satisfaction that it was a good pattern.

Carew was leaving the ends of the buried sutures free. They were long ends, long enough to fasten a dressing. Fenton wondered if that thought had occurred to Carew.

The anchoring sutures formed lines on either side of where the closure would be. They followed the line of the incision in the axillary area, anchoring both ends of the long S-shaped main incision. They formed an oval of strong stitches with trailing ends around the incision. Carew was turning to the closing of that incision now. He placed a rubber drain high up in the axillary. The careful approximation of the two edges of skin began.

Fenton bent forward to tie the sutures as Carew placed them now. He was finding himself working smoothly with Carew, finding satisfaction too in the operation now drawing to a close.

The massive area of raw muscle and tissue was becoming a smooth area of skin again, joining in the long S-shaped line of red that thinned as each skin suture went in. He watched Carew place the last suture and he bent to tie it. He straightened, grinning.

Carew *had* thought about those coaptation sutures in terms of the final dressing. He was using pressure dressings of a kind new to Fenton. He was pressing the comparatively loose axillary skin deeply into the axillary space with a line of cotton wrapped in gauze like a sausage. Carew was tying the roll in place with the loose ends of the coaptation sutures.

The roll lengthened slowly, forming an oval ridge held securely by the ends of the deeply anchored sutures and circling the whole of the operative area. Carew now filled the enclosed space with packing. The duty nurses were watching intently now; the observers in the gallery were craning their necks to peer down, talking to one another as they discussed a procedure that Fenton decided was probably as new to them as it was to him.

The secure oval of rolled cotton was becoming solid as he filled it—a raised island of sterile packing.

"Cotton combines, Nurse."

The large dressing pads came into his gloved hands and he pressed them over the whole surface, covering the rubber drain that protruded at the edge of the rolled oval. He smiled at the Chief Operating Room nurse and Miss Kline moved in to help as he began to fasten the whole pressure dressing firmly in place with a wide, elasticized bandage that involved the entire chest wall and shoulder as it was wound into place.

Fenton watched the bandage being fastened. "Very good," he said, nodding, a note of satisfaction in his voice. He looked up at the observers in the gallery rising from their seats now, gathering in groups. The interns had drawn together, obviously discussing the operation with a resident whom Fenton recognized as Bill Kendall from the GYN service.

He was surprised when he recognized Prentice talking to Dr. Cape. He glanced at the clock automatically. It was past one o'clock.

Prentice would have finished his abdominal long ago and obviously had come in to watch the last stages of the radical mastectomy. Prentice was looking down now, frowning slightly as he listened to Dr. Cape.

Fenton grinned up at them and waved a triumphant hand while he waited for Carew. He was pleased that he had taken this one with Carew. He told himself now that he had never doubted Carew's ability as he watched Prentice nod back almost disinterestedly. Cape grinned widely, the accompanying wave of his plump hand encompassing Carew and the rest of the surgical team.

Fenton looked at the tall surgeon. He was giving Miss Kline

the immediate postoperative instructions in a low voice and the anesthesiologist was listening with her, nodding approval.

Carew said, "I'll write these out for you. Thanks, Miss Kline. And thank you for a perfect anesthesia, Dr. Howarth. We'll have to watch for any collection of serum under the skin flaps and aspirate it away if it appears. We'll start shoulder movement on the fourth day. By the time healing is complete, I want her to be able to pat the top of her head easily. We'll have a look at the anchoring sutures on the fifth day. The skin sutures come out in seven days. I want to be notified at once if the arm swells. With complete axillary dissection it will probably be caused by accumulating serum, but delayed swelling could mean metastasis of the tumor."

Howarth was grinning behind his mask in satisfaction. "I kept her light. I don't expect much postoperative worry with her so far as the anesthesia goes, Dr. Carew. Are you coming through to the Recovery Room? I'll stay with her for an hour before I go to lunch."

"I have a hernia with Dr. Fenton at two," Carew said. "I'll look at her again as soon as I can get away."

"And he lunches with me first. Before the hernia," Fenton said, smiling. He pulled off his mask and shook it. He breathed deeply. The patient was being wheeled away and Fenton's eyes followed her with something close to affection. "Well," he said, as Carew joined him, "at the very least we've arrested it for Mrs. Durban, given her a breathing space. At best, we got it all and she'll get through the next five years without a recurrence, eh, Glen?"

"I certainly hope so—and I'm willing to bet on it. Statistics don't tell it all. With *plenty* of them it never comes back, and I think that may well be the case with Mrs. Durban."

"Of course," Fenton said quickly. "Of course, Glen." He glanced at Carew obliquely. Carew must know all about the statistics of cancer. Must know the percentage of five-year arrests when the lymphatic glands have not become involved. And must know that if there was involvement, if the axilla was already tainted . . .

He shook his head. Carew must know that. But there were always doctors who would not admit it was hopeless. That in the long run you could never beat it. Carew apparently was like that. Death was the enemy to Carew. Death would always be the enemy, to be fought with whatever means there were until death could no longer be held at bay. And even then, he'd still fight.

And sometimes it was men like Carew who became the great men of medicine. The pathfinders. . . .

The thought faded as he followed the direction of Carew's steady gaze. Carew was staring at the circulating nurse, already removing the scrub nurse's tray and the used instruments. The girl was tall, probably blonde—and there was something familiar about her. Fenton stared and whistled softly.

"Glen, isn't that Blake's girl? The one he locked in his private harem at the Midtown Bar?"

"I don't know about her being Blake's girl," Carew said gruffly. "But that's Jane Grant, the girl Sue Callaghan knows. The one she made a bet about with you."

"I remember." Fenton whistled softly. His eyes narrowed as Carew pulled off his surgical mask and he saw his face. The mask hung around Carew's neck loosely and he was tugging angrily at his gloves. Fenton grinned.

"Sue bet me she could attract the fair Jane into our little team to make a sixth. And of course, since Sue and you seemed to team up so well last night, Sue meant as a date for me. Right?"

"Wrong," Carew scowled.

"Which leaves me Sue?" Fenton said with pretended indignation.

"Why not? You started with her."

"Uh-huh," Fenton said. He laughed. "Good old Sue! She has everything any other girl has and uses it with less persuasion. But maybe you should persuade Sue first that that *was* what she meant. That the extra girl was for you. I mean —didn't you tell me earlier that you had a date with Sue Callaghan tonight? And then, of course, there's Paul Blake. Paul doesn't give up easily. And probably most important of all, there's the circulating Jane Grant. I mean, does she *want* to circulate? Away from the tall dark and handsome Dr. Paul Blake?"

"I'll find that out." Carew relaxed suddenly and grinned. "Just give me time, Don, just give me time!"

"Paul Blake," Fenton said thoughtfully, "is going to hate your abdominal contents."

Turning the taps over his basin, Fenton was remembering Dr. Cape and Prentice up there in the gallery suddenly, and the thought sobered him. "That's one thing I'm very sure about, Glen Carew," he thought. "Yeah. Blake is going to hate your guts all right."

Chapter Four

Afterward, Carew could not remember much about the show. There had been singing and it was set on some mythical island in the South Pacific, but that was the sum total of his knowledge.

The theater was crowded and their seats were far to the side. It wasn't long before Sue Callaghan's small, warm hand found his and pressed it to her body, gently at first, then with the growing fervor of passion.

He had been a little surprised at first. She seemed completely without inhibitions. She would love, he decided, as simply and easily as she breathed, and think very little more of it than that.

For a little while he found it amusing, then it wasn't any more. It was a game where you knew the result before you started to play. The ending was inevitable, with the climax coming as soon as they were alone. Sue was sure of it and so was he now. It took the fun out of the game.

Carew was no longer surprised when she squeezed his hand halfway through the film and bent over to whisper in his ear, her breath warm against his cheek, "Glen, take me out of here. I think I'm feverish. I need a doctor."

"I'm a doctor," he told her. "Remember?"

"Then you're just what I need, Doctor," she whispered, the

touch of her hair and her warm breath tantalizing him as she meant it to.

Glen Carew stood up, helping her. The warmth of her body touched him through their clasped hands. They walked carefully back up the aisle through the darkness toward the shadowed light above the door where a bored usherette stood with her flashlight. Their feet were silent on the thick carpet. On the wide screen, an unreal native woman in a grass skirt sang a native song in French with an American accent.

Outside, in a neighboring parking lot, as they sat together in the front seat of Carew's car, she murmured, "Glen, I'd like a drink. After that..."

Her brown eyes were almost black. In the emerald green sheath, the plunging neckline revealing the swell of her breasts and the skirt tight enough to show the curve of her hips to best advantage, she seemed to Carew to be at once slim yet voluptuous.

"I thought you needed a doctor," he said.

"I do," she husked. She was tempted to kiss him, but decided against it. You couldn't start something that you mightn't be able to stop in a parking lot, with cars coming in and out all the time.

She put her hand to her forehead. "Doctor, don't you think you should prescribe me a drink? I feel hot and awfully thirsty. It must have been the hot theater."

"No, it's us," he said. "But I'll prescribe. Let's see? Champagne? Iced, of course."

"Umm!" she said. "Residents are so much more affluent than interns. Are you taking me to Perino's, Doctor? Or the Beachcomber?"

"I might take you down San Pedro way." There was a meaningful gleam in his brown eyes. "Where the night spots are more within the bounds of a resident doctor's pay check."

"Uh-huh," she said. "I could stand that. Or maybe we could drive through to Marineland. It stays open late and I have a secret love there."

"Who?" he said jealously, pretending to stifle anger. She was good fun. He found himself liking her, for something that was more than her physical attraction.

"His name is Tommy, and I have a thing about him," she said. "He's awfully sleek and sophisticated. And every time I watch him wriggle I wish I was a lady seal."

THE DOCTOR'S PAST

He laughed with her over Tommy Tucker, Marineland's famous film star seal. Then suddenly he was wishing it was Jane Grant beside him on the seat of the Chevvy, and not Sue Callaghan at all. But just as quickly he was glad that it was not, because Jane Grant, he felt sure, would not be goddam willing. . . .

They drove down Vermont Avenue into San Pedro; he found a place where they had fairly good champagne and served it nicely from buckets of chipped ice. Sue glowed and laughed with such a note of hidden excitement that half the men in the place couldn't keep their eyes from her. So he edged her out of there, and they drove on down Vermont toward the increasing sound of the sea on a rocky coast. At Point Fermin they turned north into Palos Verdes Drive.

Only they never quite reached Marineland. Instead they drove off the road at a spot where the hills came down to the sea, and the moonlight made a track across water that was a part of the same Pacific he had known under different circumstances in a past that now seemed far behind him.

As he switched the headlights off, the sea appeared slowly, beyond a white-painted rail that glistened with dew. The sea was smooth in the moonlight, swelling, falling. . . .

"We've stopped," she said, in mock dismay.

"Did you really want to look at a seal?"

She shook her head, putting her hands up to stroke her hair with a gesture that was almost sensuous.

"Then you don't mind?" he asked softly.

"It was time we stopped running, wasn't it?"

He laughed, aware of excitement. "Was I running, Sue?"

"Maybe. But I was anyway, Glen." She turned toward him and in moonlight her eyes were black pools that he couldn't fathom. "I always run like this. And this is the way it always ends." She was breathing heavily and he could see the quick rise and fall of her breasts. "Like . . . like a sickness . . ." she muttered. "Would you say I was sick, Glen? Would you? Just because I'm here with you?"

He looked at her in consternation. "I don't get it, Sue."

"Glen, I'm not joking any more. I do need a doctor. You're nice and I'm here with you because I want to be here with you. But—"

"But what?"

"Would you say I was . . . sick? Mentally sick?" she

paused. "Would you call me a . . . a nymphomaniac? A tramp?"

"You know I wouldn't!" he said hotly.

"No," she said. "You wouldn't, would you? Not even if I was jealous and . . . selfish, and . . . and wanted you all to myself."

He frowned. "No . . ."

Her eyes glistened. "No, you wouldn't. Not if you knew I loved you, and that was what was making me that way. But *he* did."

"He?"

She nodded. "Someone I was fool enough to fall in love with not so long ago. I was a virgin, and for a while he treated me like someone very special. Only it didn't last. He wanted out then. He wanted change. Only I couldn't let him go. *I couldn't!*"

She was crying suddenly, and he had his arm around her, comforting her like a child. He started talking to her, unsure, but wanting very much to help her. Groping for the words of comfort that wouldn't seem trite.

"You're a nurse, Sue. A good nurse. I know. I've worked with you. You couldn't be . . . like that. Not even if you tried, and maybe you have been trying. You know as well as I do what nymphomania is. It isn't love, it's a disease. It's more than excessive sexual desire. It's something that eats into a woman's brain, distorting everything. Do you think you could nurse, be compassionate to the sick, if you were like that? You couldn't."

"He never sees me now. Never. Just walks past, or I see him with other girls. Once I thought I'd kill him—"

"He isn't worth thinking about, Sue. You're a nice girl, really. Look—I'll drive you back to the hospital now."

"I don't want to go back," she sobbed. "Every time I see him I remember what he said one night. He'd been trying to get rid of me, and we got in his car. . . . We drove out of town. I . . . tried to make him . . . love me. . . ."

"Forget him," he said gently. "You will in time, you know. He's not worth it. Sue—"

But she could not contain the words now that they were flowing from her. They rushed out in a flood, and Glen Carew held her tightly, feeling her trembling, sharing her emotion with her in a way he couldn't understand clearly, but feeling it just the same.

THE DOCTOR'S PAST

"Sue—" he tried to soothe her. "Never mind—"

But her words rushed on over his, feverishly.

"—He stopped the car near a wood. I remember the smell of wildflowers. He laughed at me, when I tried to kiss him. When I tried . . . to make him want me . . . he said I was . . . *like that!*" Her whole body was shaking. Carew held her tightly. "He called me all those things. The only reason he said he'd ever made love to me was because I'd wanted him to. I'd always be a little tramp, because that was what I'd always been inside me. Even before he made love to me. All I needed was the opportunity—"

"Sue," he said. "I'll drive you home—"

She didn't listen to him. The words tumbled out. "I got out of the car, and started walking. I don't know how long I walked, or where. Only I remember telling him that since he was so clever, he must be right, and I would be like that from there on—"

"Sue," he said, shaking her gently. "Sue—"

"And that's the way I've been," she said defiantly. "That's the way I *am!*"

"You're not, Sue! You wouldn't think about it like this if you were. You wouldn't let it torture you. You'd be quite unaware. Don't you see?—it just couldn't matter."

"I didn't come back to the hospital that night," she rushed on. "I remember hearing his car start. I was walking through trees. The sea wasn't far away. I meant to walk into it. I meant to drown . . . only I didn't have the courage."

"You had too much good sense," he said.

"After a while I found myself running. I climbed through a fence onto a road. After that—there's a lot I don't remember. Only—" For the first time, she hesitated, then forced herself to go on. The words came slowly now. "I remember someone being nice to me, and riding in a car. I drank whisky and there was music someplace. I remember waking in the morning—"

She had turned to him instinctively again. Carew held her gently.

"Don't talk about it, Sue," he pleaded. "You don't have to tell anyone." Only now, holding her, seeing the black eyes swollen by tears, feeling the emotion that stirred her crazily beneath his hands, he knew that she had to tell him. It was better for her that she should. There was relief in confession

—in allowing words to gush out of you and pent-up emotions to spend themselves.

"He was right, you know," she said almost in a whisper. "At heart I am just a tramp. I must be. You see, Glen, when I wakened I was in bed in a motel eighty miles up the highway. I was naked, and there was a man beside me—a man I'd never seen before—sleeping. So . . . you see?"

"You were under emotional strain," he said quietly. "You're a nurse, Sue. You've had psychiatric training. You know what happened. Compulsion—transference, perhaps. But in your case only a temporary aberration caused by emotional upset. You're an emotional woman, Sue."

"Yes," she said. "I am." Her laugh was brittle, forced. "I'm feeling emotional now, Glen."

"Don't, Sue," he said. "Not with me. Not just because you want to hurt some man you once loved. A man you still love, subconsciously. Love and hate are very close, Sue."

She was staring at him, her eyes hard and angry. "You don't want me either. I've disgusted you, haven't I? That's it."

"I was thinking of you, Sue "

"Have I?" she demanded.

"No," Carew said.

She flung herself against him. "Then help me, Glen," she whispered. "Help me. . . ."

Now, she was holding Glen Carew tightly, her nails hurting his wrists, her dark eyes wild.

"Sue," he said, "you're attractive—wonderful, but—"

"You don't want me," she flashed, releasing him.

"No," he said. "It isn't that! God, it isn't that!"

"Then why—?"

"Because you don't *have* to be like this. You're really not . . . like it at all. That's why. A virgin, you said, and you love one man, and then because he . . . turns out to be a son of a bitch—"

"You don't believe I'm what he said?" Her voice was shrill now.

"I know you're not. But Sue, can't you see that in telling me, you've made me responsible for you? You've made me your *doctor*. Sue, that's why—"

"You wouldn't want a girl you thought was like that, would you? You wouldn't . . . *kiss* a girl like that?" The words were almost a scream. He shook her.

"No. But you're not like that. You have to convince your-

THE DOCTOR'S PAST

self that you're not. You should leave Los Angeles. Go someplace where you're not known. Where there are no memories to torture you. Start again, Sue. All men aren't like that. You'll find one who'll love you for what you are, for what you can be, and..."

She became strangely quiet.

"If you kissed me," she said. "I'd know you meant that. And maybe I'd believe it too. I'll try. I'll try."

"All right!" he said hoarsely. "All right! I'll kiss you, Sue, if that's what you want!"

"Please, Glen! Please..."

Her face moved close to him with those dark eyes wide. Her voice was low, exciting as she pleaded. Glen Carew looked at her, saw her trembling, feeling her need very clearly. And there was the same urgency within himself, expanding, driving away reason, teaching, control. The lost years propelled him violently....

His mouth crushed down upon hers. He felt her body arch crazily toward him.

"Please, Glen. Please..." Her voice murmured on, urgent, compelling.

He fumbled, and she drew him on; warm, demanding, her face wet with tears, her lips whispering constantly as though she could not control them.

Then her breathless whispering stopped, the words becoming lost entirely in desire. But a single word escaped her before she stilled....

"Paul!"

Later, Glen Carew would think about that single word torn from the depth of remembered passion, from other emotion that had seemed like nightmare. But she had quietened now. She was lying still in his arms, her face pressed against his shoulder, hidden. But he could feel her tears.

She moved within the circle of his arms. When he looked at her, she was no longer crying.

"You can take me back now, Glen," she said, smiling. "It was what you wanted to do all along, wasn't it? Take me back?"

"I only meant to kiss you, Sue!" he said, embarrassed.

She nodded. "I know. Only it isn't always easy to stop. It's no different with a girl, either."

"I'm sorry, Sue...."

She shook her head and sat up. "Don't be sorry. I'm

not, Glen, because I'm remembering all the things you said. You're right, I *know* that now. I'm going to... go away."

His voice was hoarse. "I don't think I want you to go away. Not any more."

"Glen, Nature gave me a lovely body, I know. But it isn't enough." She turned away from him. "There's truth in the things you said. I'm going to try to forget, Glen. If I go away, maybe I will forget. Maybe I'll even find someone as you said, but it won't be you. You deserve a nice girl, Glen."

"And you're a nice girl," he said firmly.

She reached up and kissed him quickly. "Thank you, Glen! Maybe I can still be that. I'm going to try. But maybe... I just don't have the moral strength any more. So... I couldn't do *that* to you. Not to the first man who's really been kind to me. You'd get hurt. I don't want that." She laughed suddenly. "Go find yourself a girl like the girl I was once! I'd help you find her if I could." She groped for her handbag and pulled out a small gold compact. She began powdering her nose. He switched on the light in the ceiling of the car.

"Sue, you must listen—"

"Take me back to the hospital, Glen. I've made up my mind. I'm going East, soon. Back to where I started out as a girl with ideas of dedication to the profession of nursing." The dark eyes were no longer black, but a soft brown.

"Okay," he said. He switched on the ignition.

She was almost silent during the long drive back to the hospital. For a few moments they sat quietly in his car outside the nurses' residence. Around them the night life of a great hospital went on imperturbably. Dim lights shone in the silent wards where duty nurses talked in low voices. Two white-coated residents crossed the open space between two buildings hurriedly, each with a stethoscope about his neck.

Outside the entrance to the Emergency Room an ambulance stood with open doors.

Carew said, "Shall I see you tomorrow, Sue?"

"If you do, it won't mean anything, Glen," she said slowly. "But I'll say good-bye before I leave. Maybe in a week."

"At the Midtown Bar?"

"No. I won't be going there any more."

"You're sure about all this? That you want to go?"

She laughed softly. In some ways, she decided as she

THE DOCTOR'S PAST

studied him, Glen Carew was very boyish. She leaned across and kissed him quickly again.

"I'm sure, Glen! And I'm grateful because it was your suggestion, remember?" She opened the door and slipped out. "Thank you for everything! If I could have a wish, I'd wish that I could have met you first, and not... someone else."

"Sue—"

"I'm sorry." She started to run. Carew called after her, but she kept on running. He watched her slim figure disappear in the shadow of the entrance to the nurses' home before he jabbed at the starter angrily.

"What's the matter with you, Carew?" he asked himself. "You should be grateful to her. For what happened. You didn't lose anything, except a little of the debt owed to you for a lot of lost years. So what the hell?"

Only there was no contentment. There was only sadness, and a heavy feeling that was like loss....

He drove the car down the drive, and went up wearily to bed.

There was work tomorrow. Work, he knew, could be a panacea for all ills. And he had learned something today. Women weren't much different from men. He had learned it in the surgery when his scalpel parted the skin of a woman's breast. And he had learned it again tonight, in another woman's arms.

Sue Callaghan did not need him and he did not need her—or any other woman.

Only suddenly, as he climbed the stairs and walked along the passage past the entrances to the individual quarters of the resident doctors, he found himself thinking of Jane Grant and Paul Blake.

He cursed softly as he opened his door. He was still thinking of them as he fell asleep.

But in the morning the work of a great hospital caught him up, and there was no more time for personal thought. The surgical schedules were long and arduous, and now, abruptly, he was getting a full share of them. More than a full share. He lost Fenton as his assistant. Fenton moved to another team. He acquired Tom Linton, a dark-haired young man with a flashing smile and the shoulders of a college athlete.

He liked Linton, but Linton had neither Fenton's background of a former brief friendship with something shared, nor Fenton's ability as a surgeon. Jeff Wilson was also a permanent adjunct to Carew's surgical team, it seemed. The tall, thin figure of the intern appeared invariably each time he scrubbed for an operation. At Midtown General Hospital the interns in the surgical service formed a pool, upon which individual resident surgeons could draw as they needed help.

Only nobody called on Wilson, if another intern was available. So, Wilson chose to scrub in at Carew's side every chance he got. And after a while Carew became accustomed to those curious brown eyes watching him, the questions the intern was learning to confine to occasions when they scrubbed together or treated patients on the surgical floor.

And almost unobtrusively, Wilson was becoming a good assistant, so that Carew found himself giving Wilson retractors to hold, ordering him to clip bleeders that should have been the responsibility of the slower and less interested first assistant, Tom Linton.

These things meant greater responsibility for Glen Carew.

He saw Jane Grant often in that first week in the operating room, hovering just outside the area of sterile white light. But her clear eyes had acquired a look that was almost hostile when their eyes met now. Invariably, she looked away, disdainfully, leaving him embarrassed.

He puzzled about that new look in Jane Grant's eyes, but could not find an answer to it. Not unless Sue—?

But Sue Callaghan seemed to have disappeared, and the long schedules of surgery that a coldly polite Dr. Prentice was arranging for him, each case invariably needing Recovery Room attention later, left him no opportunity to visit the Midtown Bar nights with Don Fenton and the other residents.

It appeared that the schedules were being arranged deliberately by Dr. Prentice for that purpose, and his resentment grew.

He was working in the small office at the end of the male postoperative ward when the door opened and he looked up to see Fenton grinning at him from the doorway.

"So this is where you've been hiding?" Fenton said. "Haven't seen you all week. Mind if I come in?"

"Help yourself," Carew said wearily. But Fenton's smile was contagious. He pushed the pile of papers aside and reached for a cigarette from the pack Fenton was offering.

"I know how insistent Sue can be, but I haven't known her victims to disappear entirely for a week, before."

"I haven't seen Sue," Carew said soberly, remembering.

"Well, neither have I, come to think of it," Fenton said. "And that isn't like her. Mostly, she follows up." His glance was speculative. "You didn't quarrel?"

Carew shook his head. "No. Why should we?"

"Nobody needs to quarrel with Sue. Not if they're male and normal. Nothing to quarrel about," Fenton said.

"She's not—!" Carew started defensively. He stopped.

Fenton chuckled. "Sue is okay, Glen. Unfortunate, maybe —but I like her too. I've often thought her restlessness has some psychological basis. But that's not *my* worry. She's attractive and generous. What more can you want? Like me to fix up a night at the Midtown tonight? Diane can tell Sue and between them they can find a third girl. Morganthal has to work, but I can get Linton to make the six. How about that?"

Carew frowned. "I have a cholecystectomy at the end of the schedule. That means a stint in the Recovery Room. Sorry—"

"Prentice said you wouldn't be on call the first week and this is still the first week."

Carew nodded. "Prentice *said* that. But Prentice also seems to resent his residents going out nights. So this seems to be the way it works out. The last patient on the schedule always needs Recovery Room attention. So..."

Fenton grunted. "You ever heard of covering?"

Carew frowned. "Of course! But—"

"Okay. You're not on call. The chore really isn't yours anyway and someone offers to cover for you. So?"

"Who'd be that crazy?" Carew asked doubtfully.

"Morg would do it like a shot. He's on call, but it only means that he'd have to find someone else to take over your patient *if* he happened to be called. And the patient would only need attention for an hour or so coming out of the anesthesia. It's hardly likely that he'd get a call in that time. But even if he did, Morg could handle it."

"But it is my patient," Carew protested, frowning.

"For Crissake!" Fenton said. "What are you?—dedicated or something?"

Carew shrugged. "Okay, okay, Don! I'll come along, if you can swing it."

"Consider it swung," Fenton said. "You can depend on it. See you around eight at the Midtown. We'll be there earlier than that, so you'll have to find your own way. Whoever I dig up for the cover will see you in the Recovery Room after dinner. Right?"

"Right," Carew said.

"And don't take any short cuts to get to the Midtown," Fenton warned him solemnly. "I'll expect you there in one piece. Sue would be furious if you arrived with any essential parts missing."

"If Sue comes along," he said.

Fenton stared at him. "*If?* Man, you don't know that girl so well after all! I'd make a bet, except that it's a shame to take money from the innocent. Sue mightn't turn up? Ye Gods! You're thinking of someone else, Glen. Not Sue Callaghan."

He went out shaking his head sadly. The door closed, and Carew turned back to study the reports on the afternoon's surgical cases.

He tried to read them, knowing that he must. Knowing that the typed and written notes were knowledge that he must absorb to perform surgery the way each of the subjects of the notes needed it. But the words kept blurring and he could neither retain their substance nor make decisions. His mind kept returning to Sue Callaghan and unaccountably to another girl, as fair as Sue was dark. As opposite from Sue, he was sure, as black from white. A girl who looked at him now for some reason that he couldn't understand with eyes that were cold and disinterested. . . .

The image of a girl blurred. It was neither one nor the other, but a little of each, and therefore it lost significance. It was frustrating. It puzzled him, until he forced the invading questions from his mind.

He gained concentration slowly, with effort.

He began to think as a doctor again.

Chapter Five

"I don't expect any trouble with her," Carew said. He smiled at Morganthal, doodling on the office blotter with someone else's pencil. "Pulmonary complications are always a possibility with upper abdominal surgery. And there's some reduction of respiration. If you're called away, the nurse mustn't leave her."

"Don't worry," Morganthal said, smiling his broad, friendly smile. He heaved his bulk off the corner of the desk and put down the pencil. "I've arranged with Howarth to take over if I'm called. But it looks like it'll be a quiet night."

Carew nodded, pleased. The anesthesiologist would be better than a surgeon in here if the woman breathing heavily on the bed in the Recovery Room had trouble. An anesthesiologist was specially trained to handle postoperative complications. And Howarth was a good man in his specialty.

"If that's okay with Howarth, it's fine with me too, Doctor."

"Dave, dammit!" Morganthal said. "Not Doctor! And Bob Howarth doesn't mind. He's reading up on something and he can do it in here as well as anywhere. Chances are I won't need him though. Think of me when you get there. And don't feel too grateful—I'll get back at you one night when I need a cover, okay?"

"Any night," Carew said, smiling.

He was walking to the door when the phone rang. He waited, frowning, while Morganthal picked up the receiver.

"Recovery Room," Morganthal said. Then his expression changed, brightening, and he grinned. "Dave Morganthal, Sue. Yes, Glen's still here. But what are *you* doing hanging around the hospital? I thought you'd have gone with the others long ago." He listened, and laughed. He put the phone down. "Glen, it's for you. Sue Callaghan! I'll have another look at our patient. Have fun."

He walked past Glen Carew, and went out into the big room. Carew could hear him joking with the duty nurse as he picked up the phone.

"Glen?"

He said, "Hello, Sue. Where have you been hiding?"

"I changed shifts with another girl. It wasn't hard to do, hers was the graveyard shift. Eleven till seven-thirty." Her laugh was a little forced.

"To avoid me?" he asked, frowning.

She was silent for a moment before she answered. "Yes, Glen. But not because I don't—like you. I do. Only, I keep remembering the things you said. I'm trying to act on your advice, Doctor." She concluded lightly, but there seemed an undercurrent of sadness in her voice. She added quickly as he considered that in silence, "I suppose you've heard that I've carried out the first part of your advice already?"

"I haven't heard anything," he said. "I've been too damned busy to listen. My chief sees to that. What have you done?"

"I've resigned, Glen. I move out tomorrow. I thought you knew."

"Well, I didn't!" He scowled at the phone, remembering. *Then* it had seemed good advice. It still did. But... He said, "Sue, you're sure that you want to do this?"

"Yes, I am. You were right, Glen. I'll be grateful to you some day for that. That's something I know deep down. But in the meantime, no dates for Sue. She's a changed girl."

"Where will you go?" he asked.

"Home. And that's a word I haven't used for a long time," she said sadly. "It means a New England mother and father. It means... well, that I'll have time to think about myself and maybe find out what's happened to the girl who used to live with them... a long time ago."

THE DOCTOR'S PAST

"Nothing's happened to her," he said. "You'll find she's still the same."

Her voice broke a little. "I think I'll find she's a stranger I've got to get to know and understand all over again, Glen."

"You'll go back to nursing?"

"Maybe, a month, a year, what's time? I'll go back if the new me feels the need to put on her uniform again."

"She will—and it will work out for you, Sue."

"Keep your fingers crossed," she said lightly.

"I think Fenton and the others are expecting you at the Midtown," he said. "Why not let's say good-bye there? You'll have the good wishes of all your friends to take along."

She hesitated momentarily. "I'm sorry, Glen. I can't trust myself—not yet. And there's another reason. Diane asked me about tonight. I told her, no. I... arranged for someone else to take my place. I found another date for you, Glen."

"A blind date?" he said doubtfully.

"You'll like her. She's more your type."

"Who is?"

"You'll find out when you get there. I'm not going to tell you anything about her, except that she's attractive and a... a nice girl. Good-bye, Glen."

"Wait," he said frowning. "Will I hear from you? If I can ever help you?"

"You have helped me," she said. "A great deal. Good-bye, Glen." She tried to keep her voice steady. "And thanks for everything."

The phone clicked before he could reply. He held the receiver, staring at it, frowning, feeling lonely.

"Good-bye, Sue," he said softly into the empty phone. "And good luck."

He put the receiver down slowly.

Standing at a window in one of the female postoperative wards, Dr. Cape, Midtown's medical superintendent, rubbed his ear thoughtfully as he watched Dr. Glen Carew walking quickly across the parking lot toward the house doctors' residence.

He said to Dr. Prentice, who was examining a patient

in the bed behind him, "I think you said Dr. Carew was in the Recovery Room, eh?"

"Carew? Yes, he is. The last operation on his schedule was a cholecystectomy. Dr. Carew's duties ended officially when he concluded the operation, but naturally he'd stay with her."

"Naturally," Cape said. He rubbed his ear and smiled at Glen Carew's tall figure as it receded hurriedly up the steps of the residence. "Dr. Carew isn't on call, is he?"

"No. The first week is always free."

"Except for possible complications following surgery, of course?"

"Of course."

Cape came back heavily to the bed, to beam down at the patient Prentice was examining. "Well, and how is our Mrs. Durban tonight?"

"I feel fine, Doctor," the woman on the bed said. She looked weakly from one man to the other. "Dr. Carew started me on arm movements yesterday. I can raise my arm to my shoulder already."

Cape said, "That's fine! Don't overdo it though. Just do what Dr. Carew tells you. No more." He glanced at Prentice. "Her arm appears swollen?"

Prentice nodded. "It is. But as I was just saying to Mrs. Durban, early swelling is a good sign. So far as possible metastasis is concerned, I don't think we're going to have much worry. The swelling should start to abate in a few more days. It's quite a common postoperative symptom when the axillary dissection has been complete. Dr. Carew removed the whole mass of tissue, including the lymphatic glands. He removed the axillary mattress sutures today and the skin flaps were adherent."

"Any accumulation of serum in the axilla?"

Prentice studied the chart in his hand briefly. "Dr. Carew aspirated a pocket of serum from the axilla on Wednesday. None apparent since."

Cape nodded cheerfully. "That's fine! How do you feel, Mrs. Durban?"

The patient smiled, the tightening of skin making the powdering of freckles across her nose stand out against the pallor of sickness. As she listened to the two men, she had formed the impression that in some way she couldn't

THE DOCTOR'S PAST

understand clearly, Dr. Carew was on trial here. She resented that.

She said firmly, "I'm weak, of course, and I have pain when I move my arm. But I didn't expect to feel as well as this. Dr. Carew has been wonderful!"

Cape glanced at Prentice, but the service chief's face was expressionless. "That's what I like to hear, Mrs. Durban," Cape said. "A patient with faith in her doctor is well on the way to convalescence. Don't you agree, Dr. Prentice?"

Prentice said quickly, "Yes, of course." He added, "I'm more than satisfied with Mrs. Durban's progress. She'll have to come and see us for quite a long while after she's discharged from the hospital, and have regular checks. X-rays, pathological tests. We're going to make sure that Dr. Carew's good work isn't allowed to be wasted. Right, Mrs. Durban?"

"Dr. Carew is a very good doctor," the woman said quietly.

"He is, indeed!" Cape agreed heartily. His glance at Prentice was slightly malicious. "Did you know that you were Dr. Carew's first patient here at Midtown, Mrs. Durban? And here you are, a convalescing example of Dr. Carew's ability. Dr. Carew has an international reputation as a surgeon. He was in charge of reconstructive surgery in a famous military hospital before he came to us."

"Yes," she said, mollified. "I heard two of the nurses talking about him one day. They said that."

"Now, before we leave you, is there anything at all worrying you about the operation, Mrs. Durban? If there is, we'd like to know about it, and maybe we can help you."

She shook her head slowly, her red hair massed against the white pillow. "No. I've every confidence in Dr. Carew. At first I was worried. I... felt one-sided. I wondered about my husband.... But Dr. Carew explained how I'd be fitted for—an artificial breast contained in a bra. After that, I didn't feel so bad. I don't suppose I should have thought of that. I mean ... just being alive ... being healthy again ... I should be satisfied. But a woman has her pride about these things."

"You'll be as attractive as ever, my dear," Cape said. "Your husband will still be proud of you. Does she have sedation tonight, Doctor?"

Prentice frowned. "Nurse! Mrs. Durban can have her sedation now. We want her to rest. Good night, Mrs. Durban."

"Good night."

Seated in the chair in Prentice's office, Dr. Cape lit a cigarette. He said, "Well?"

"I can't fault Dr. Carew's work as a surgeon," Prentice said slowly. "But then, I've never doubted that. Have you?"

Cape grunted. "I've never doubted anything about him. Did I give you that impression?"

"You know damned well you did! You asked me for my opinion. I've been trying to form one, because you asked."

"You would've anyway, Stanley," Cape said, grinning, "since surgery is your service. I suppose you realize that we're going to have to give him Blake's job? With the qualifications and the surgical ability Carew has, we can't do anything else."

"But not yet," Prentice said, frowning.

"Because you still haven't made up your mind what kind of man Carew is—apart from surgery?"

"Yes."

"Come down out of the clouds, Stanley," Cape said. "I've known some bastards in my time who were good doctors, and better executives. What manner of man is Blake?"

Prentice frowned. "I know all about Blake. But this thing is different. Carew is different."

"Think Carew could fall apart, eh? Because you think he might want to play? To get away from what's behind him? Well, suppose he does? Suppose we let him get it out of his system? He could still be a better man for that. It happens." He squinted at Prentice thorough half-closed eyes. "You see any signs?"

Prentice shook his head. "I've given him schedules that gave him Recovery Room work afterward. Like tonight. He resents it, but he does it."

"Suppose he was to take some time off, leaving someone to cover for him? He's not on call, Stanley. The only thing involved is his moral obligation to his patient, and if he had that taken care of—what would you think? Would you view it as the first symptom of deterioration?"

Prentice rubbed his eyes wearily. Finally he said, "I don't know what I'd think. I just want a little more time. I hope you're right about him, and it all works out. Damn

THE DOCTOR'S PAST

it—I can't help liking Carew. But I keep thinking of the years of discipline behind him, and I keep wondering what the result might be. I keep searching for the reason why he's here, too...."

"So we wait a little while. We keep an open mind. We see what happens?"

"Yes."

"All right. We wait," Cape said. He heaved his bulk out of the chair and breathed heavily as he stubbed the cigarette. "But don't force him into anything, Stanley," he said quietly. "One of these days you'll be running a hospital yourself. You'll find your medical staff vary a lot, but you can still organize them into an efficient machine to run your hospital. You'll come across the incorruptibles, like yourself. But you'll find the others too. Like Blake, self-opinionated, conceited, without any moral misgivings outside medicine. Like Fenton, brilliant, but content to cruise so long as life remains pleasant for him. Or like Glen Carew—running away from something, and maybe not quite sure what, or why. You'll meet 'em all, Stanley. And you'll have to learn to live with them, to use them to your best advantage as I do. It doesn't matter greatly about their private lives, just so long as you *can* use them the way you want."

"If I ever do run the medical staff of a hospital," Prentice said, "it will be with staff I'll choose myself."

"Sure, Stanley," Cape said, gesturing with a plump head. "Sure you will! And after you've chosen them, you'll still have my problems while doctors are human beings. You'll have the Blakes, the Fentons, the Carews. You'll have the dedicated and the casual. You'll have the lazy, the disinterested, the careless. You'll probably even have someone who's just like yourself—so far above reproach that you'll sometimes wonder if he's human. And you never know, that might be someone like Carew. Someone you were prepared to write off as a loss because you doubted his motives."

The Midtown Bar was hazed with smoke. The seating at the Midtown resembled church pews, each pair of which enclosed a table. And only at the far end of the long room were there the conventional tables and chairs designed for couples or single customers.

Originally, the Midtown Bar and Grill had had a very mixed clientele, but gradually the management, in the heavily muscled person of Fred Champion who owned the place, had realized that the neighboring hospital could be good business.

They could be even better business, Fred decided, if his bar was really respectable. So he'd put in what he considered were better fixtures, and with the help of two burly gentlemen he'd known in the Marines he'd gradually discouraged the original nondescript and transient patrons.

Now, the occasional overpainted girl who strayed in with an eye on the hospital male medical staff did not stay long. Neither did the young men in jeans and shirts from the alleys behind the hospital, even though many of them carried switchblade knives and had been known to use them. Fred knew them all by sight and type, and had no fears about any of them. Some left protesting—but they left, one way or another.

The bums, the drunks, the derelicts learned very quickly from Fred and his two hard-eyed waiters that their presence was no longer desired.

Within weeks after Fred had finished redecorating, the dribble of hospital staff coming in when off duty increased to a steady and profitable flood. In a couple of months, Fred was seriously considering buying the shop next door and extending his overcrowded premises to hold them all.

Now a different language was heard in the Midtown. The jargon of the hospital, instead of back alley talk. At first Fred Champion had found it as incomprehensible as the slang of the tough customers he'd had when he came to the Midtown from the Marines in '45.

But gradually he caught on. He learned to reply in kind. And to evaluate the different levels in hospital society.

They all came here. Student nurses, R.N.'s, laboratory workers, domestic staff, laundry staff, orderlies, and ambulance drivers. He began to learn the difference between the interns who teetered defiantly on the lower rungs of the hierarchy of medicine, full of theory but still hesitant to apply it, and the resident doctors with their specialties, and their confidence born of experience.

Some Fred liked at first sight, like the man walking in

THE DOCTOR'S PAST 61

now, although he had only seen him once before. Others he disliked, although he did not let them see it. He was too good a businessman for that.

The man coming in, staring through the smoke as though in search of someone, was new at Midtown. But Fred knew all about him. Fred had heard of Colonel Carew, and so had both of his friends busy down at the other end of the room with trays of drinks and food from the kitchen. They knew that Colonel Carew had got most of the bad ones from Okinawa, and, much later, from Korea.

"Evening, Colonel," Fred said, his homely face parting in a grin. "You looking for someone?"

Carew had turned involuntarily. He returned the smile of the solid, jolly-looking man behind the bar and was not deceived by its gentleness. Fred Champion, he decided, was tough. Those ridges over his eyes had been made by fists that had scarred tissue there. And the puckered scar on one of the thick forearms below the short white sleeves of his coat could only have been put there by a bullet.

Carew said, "Not Colonel any more. Just Doctor now, Fred. We haven't met professionally before, have we?"

"I managed to avoid it," Fred said with a chuckle.

"You were luckier than some."

"I'll bet!" Fred said with feeling. "Can I help you now, Colonel?—Doc?"

"I was looking for Dr. Fenton."

Fred jerked his head toward the other end of the room. "They're up there. Last table. I'll send along a round of drinks. I know what the others drink. How about you? Whisky?"

"Scotch. With water and ice. It's hot outside."

"Not as hot as Okinawa though, eh, Doc?" Fred said. "This round is on the house."

"Why?"

Fred shrugged. "I had some buddies met you on that little slice of hell. You're welcome, Doc. I'll tell the boys to look after you, and your party. You get the best service we've got. Not just tonight—any time."

Carew muttered thanks and walked on, embarrassed. There was always someone who remembered. Even here. ... Couldn't they realize that he wanted to forget it all?

"Last cubicle on the right, Doctor," Fred called after

him, helpfully. "You want anything special, you just order. If we haven't got it, we'll get it for you."

Carew walked away quickly. He slowed as a white-coated man spoke to him and he recognized Jeff Wilson. Other interns, residents spoke to him. A nurse smiled and nodded.

His uneasiness faded, but he had forgotten what Sue had said about finding a date for him until Fenton called from a cubicle on his right.

"In here, Glen."

He had almost walked past. He turned quickly, but he didn't see a grinning Fenton, or Fenton's companion, Diane Foster. The third occupant of the cubicle was Jane Grant, looking at him with steady gray-green eyes that suddenly became embarrassed and looked away as he stared at her.

"At last the prodigal," Fenton laughed. "And don't stare at her, man! She's your date! Didn't Sue tell you?"

Glen Carew shook his head. He sat down carefully and looked at Jane. She had a lot of color in her face, it had flooded there when he stared at her. But he didn't care.

He smiled involuntarily. She looked as she had that other night with Blake. She had the same dress on, but she was wearing it for him—as his date.

"I hope this is all right with you, Miss Grant?"

She looked at him deliberately. With that heightened color, that brightness in her eyes, she was lovely. Her closeness left Carew a little breathless.

She said slowly, "I'm not on any blind date, Doctor. Sue asked me if I would take her place tonight as your date. I promised her I would. I wanted to ride out to the airport with her, but she said she'd rather I . . . came here. But of course, if you—"

He stopped her quickly, "I'm delighted, Miss Grant. I just thought—"

"For Crissake!" Fenton said. "Take off your stuffed shirt, feller! She answers to the name of Jane. Sorry about Linton—Prentice put him on call tonight at the last minute, so it's just a foursome. Anyway, you can see enough of Linton in the operating room. I'll get you a drink—" He broke off as a waiter brought a tray of glasses to the table. What's this, Pete? Someone order?"

"With compliments from the boss for Colonel Carew's party," the waiter said conspiratorially. "This one is on the

THE DOCTOR'S PAST

house. And Fred said he bought a batch of steaks this mornin' that made him drool just lookin'. Says he bets you never get steak like it at the hospital. If you feel like a steak supper—I'm to make sure they come from the special batch, for your table."

"Now I've heard everything!" Fenton said. "This comes of going out with celebrities, like the Colonel here. Make four, Pete! Tell the boss we'll come again."

"Any time you're with the Colonel," Pete said, "you get the works!"

"Well," Fenton said when he had gone, "it mightn't be as good as the sukiyaki we've had in Tokyo, Colonel, but it should be better than the automat, *or* the hospital."

"The Midtown Bar and Grill is going to lose itself a customer if anyone else around here calls me Colonel," Carew said. "I *told* him!"

"Old habits," Fenton said. "Believe it or not, Glen, I find myself thinking of you as Major most of the time. But Fred and his boys will soon catch on. They're good guys."

The conversation eddied, with Fenton joking with Diane. She had a soft, musical laugh. Carew turned to his own companion.

"You must have been awfully young for such a high rank, Doctor?" Jane said, her gray-green eyes curious.

"I happened to be a specialist," he said shortly. "They put me in charge of a department of the hospital and had to give me rank."

"Then you had the experience," she said. "What's more, you don't like talking about it. Paul warned me you were a little touchy on that subject."

He frowned. "Blake?"

"Yes. Paul Blake."

Anger flashed briefly in his brown eyes. "Since we're on personal things—I've been wondering why you're here tonight? And *not* out with Blake?"

She frowned, her dark brows drawing together. Her rather full lips compressed slightly. "All right. It was something Sue told me. I decided to cut my losses." She made it light. "And don't ask me what it was. That's a secret between friends."

"Have you told Blake it's . . . off?"

She shook her head. For a moment her eyes were worried. "I meant to call him tonight. He's in charge of the surgical floor for the evening shift." She shrugged. "I decided to save it until the next time he asks me for a date. If he does. Maybe he won't."

"He will," Carew said. "He doesn't give up easily."

She looked at him quickly. "That's what Sue said. But it doesn't matter what Paul Blake says, I'm not going out with him again. Ever."

Carew played with his glass. "Mind if I say I'm glad of that?"

"Why should I?"

"We meet every day in the O.R. I've seen you there each day, but you never seemed to see me. In fact I was beginning to think you had some strong reason for disliking me."

"Before we met? How could I?"

He glanced at her, but her eyes were downcast.

"*I* don't feel as though we are meeting for the first time. Or that this is our first date. Does that seem strange to you, Jane?"

She looked up at him slowly, her eyes darker than he had seen them. "No," she said. "It doesn't seem strange to me. I felt the same. As though I'd known you before. I felt it the first time I cáme here with Paul. It was raining, and ... you talked to Paul at the bottom of the steps. I looked back, and you were watching me. I wanted to meet you then. Only afterward—" She broke off.

"Paul Blake monopolized you and there was Sue?"

"Yes," she said. "There was Sue. I like her. I think I got to know her better than anyone else in the time I've been here. I felt sorry for Sue, and angry with you. I resented you. I resented what a date with you might do to her."

He looked away. "If Sue warned you against me, as well as against Blake, she was probably right," he said gloomily. "But you're here. I don't understand that."

She laughed softly. "You don't know very much about women, do you? I'm here because I wanted to come. I can look after myself—I'm not Sue." She smiled secretly. "You'd be flattered if you knew some of the things she said about you. I think she was on the way to falling in love with you. But she was going away from here. She'd made up her mind about that. So ... she wanted us to meet."

"I advised her to go away."

She nodded. "I know. And you were right. She told me

THE DOCTOR'S PAST

some of the things you said. But I don't want to talk about that, Glen. It's something that happened before we met."

"I wish we could have met sooner," he said quietly. "Can you believe that, Jane?"

"Hey, there!" Fenton said across the table. "Is that a private conversation, or can anyone join in?"

Carew smiled. Over the words, he watched Jane Grant smile and nod. He had come here to relieve the tensions, to escape the demands of hospital. But suddenly the night had assumed a new significance, a new meaning.

"I was saying," Fenton said, "although you two were too far away to hear me, that we should hold our New Year's Eve party right here in Fred's this year. Last year we had it in an apartment over in the next block. Henson's apartment. Henson was, of all things, a *married* intern. Moved to San Francisco General at the end of his internship. All the off-duty staff in the surgical service went to the party—medics and nurses. We kept it in the family, surgical service only—but the apartment was so damned crowded there wasn't room for respectable incest."

"Don't say *you* didn't try," Diane laughed.

Carew said, "New Year?"

"Sure," Fenton said. "'And New Year is just six weeks off. Time to start planning, if we want the party to be a success. Pity Sue won't be around. That gal was always interesting."

"What about me?" Diane asked, pouting. "And what could we do in this place?"

"Everything about you, honey," Fenton said grinning, "is exactly right. And what we couldn't do here, we could do elsewhere."

The conversation became general then. The steak arrived for a late supper and they sat on, drinking and talking, reluctant to leave as the Midtown Bar emptied slowly. Afterward, they walked back together slowly, still as a foursome, the conversation fading as they approached the hospital. In the lighted windows above them as they walked through the gates, the graveyard shift was just settling in, with the clock above the entrance showing a little after eleven. Above them an occasional figure passed a lighted window.

Fenton said soberly, "If we were in Tokyo, we'd be walking back into quarters after daylight, Glen. Not this early."

"You can't turn back time," Carew said. "Even if you want to. And who does?"

"I do!" Fenton said. "Every time I'm called to an emergency in the middle of the night. Or when I'm with a patient *in extremis*—" He broke off abruptly. "Now what the hell made me say that? Diane, you're going to have to brighten me up before we part. I know a seat over on the lawn among the shrubs."

"I'll bet you do!" Diane said. She looked at Jane Grant. "Do you think I should, Jane?"

"No." Jane smiled. "But you'll go just the same."

"I'm just a weak girl," Diane said, laughing. "No resistance."

Carew watched them walk across the small lawn. In the corner where visitors sometimes waited on the bench there, they sat down, and their indistinct shadows merged abruptly. Carew looked down at the girl beside him.

She said quickly, "Thanks for this evening, Glen. I'll remember it—"

His touch on her arm stopped her and under his hand he could feel her trembling suddenly.

"Does it have to end here? Tonight?"

"No—not unless you want it to." Her voice sounded softer, a little breathless.

"Then we'll have other nights together?"

"Yes." It was no more than a whisper. "We'll have ... other nights."

"Good night, Jane."

She turned slowly and he kissed her. She had a moment of detached resistance that was instinctive. You didn't kiss here in front of the nurses' residence where any nurse who happened to look out one of the windows could see you. Still, she *was* kissing him, and stronger feeling that she had fought off when other men, other boys, had kissed her, possessed her and would not be denied, so that it was Carew who released her and stepped back.

"I'll see you tomorrow in the O.R.," he said breathlessly. "Do you mind if I tell you that you're the first girl I've ever known who looks beautiful in a scrub dress?"

She looked at him, confused.

He smiled. "Tomorrow, Jane, we'll plan a date?"

"Tomorrow ..." she managed to say.

She ran up the steps, aware of his eyes watching her.

THE DOCTOR'S PAST

She fled into the shadows at the bend of the passage where he couldn't see her and leaned against the wall momentarily, her young heart thudding, her mind and senses in a turmoil while she waited for the crisp sound of his footsteps on concrete as he walked away.

"I believe I want to love you, Glen Carew!" she thought in astonishment.

And that was something that she couldn't understand. She hadn't felt this need to give before with any man. But one evening wasn't enough time to fall in love. It couldn't be that.

Chapter Six

Glen Carew walked slowly from the operating suite toward the postoperative wards where dressing rounds were almost due. His dark brows were drawn in a frown. He had just come from a difficult inguinal hernia operation that had heavily taxed his skill as a surgeon. Yet, the operation should not have been so wearing. Nor should he feel as he did now, with this feeling of doubt, the thought that he should have concluded the operation more quickly, more efficiently.

He scowled at the familiar figure of Dr. Stanley Prentice down at the end of the corridor stepping into the elevator. Prentice had walked in to observe the conclusion of the operation. The surgical chief had kept glancing from the clock to the tense surgical team around the table. Prentice had gone out again before Carew had supervised the final dressing, and the service chief's face had been quite expressionless.

Carew knew that Prentice had thought the operation too drawn out. And if Prentice had suggested that, he would not have been able to deny it. He *had* taken too long. The transversalis fascia had been of such poor quality that he had had to use the Farris technique unexpectedly. And he had difficulty in remembering it in the necessary minute detail.

He swore under his breath as he walked toward the

wards. His concentration had been bad, and last night had been the reason.

He should have stayed in the residence last night to read up the Farris technique. It had been a long time since he had repaired an inguinal hernia and he had suspected that the weakness of the fascia was pronounced.

Pronounced? It had been ready to fall apart! God, it had been—!

He had taken too long for the repair. There had been more blood loss than usual, and consequently there would be more postoperative shock. Linton hadn't seemed to notice the passing of time, or his difficulty in achieving the complete concentration that he had needed. But Prentice hadn't missed a damned thing. And somehow Prentice had learned that he had gone out last night, although he hadn't said anything. Prentice had just stood there observing, expressionless— missing nothing.

"To hell with Dr. Prentice!" he thought bitterly. "If he wants me to stay in the hospital, why doesn't he put me on call? And he can't say that the gall bladder patient needed *me*. She had Morganthal, with Howarth on call if she needed resuscitation."

And she hadn't needed resuscitation, or any help at all other than nursing and mild sedation. So what the hell?

It took effort to force those disturbing thoughts from his mind, to shake off a feeling that was close to guilt. It had been a bad morning, he admitted. But that was all. It had started when he had walked, gowned, masked, and gloved, to the operating table and his eyes had sought the eyes of the circulating nurse who should have been there waiting for the entry of the surgeon and his assistants.

The circulating nurse's eyes had been brown instead of gray-green, and the figure beneath the scrub dress heavy, almost shapeless. The nurse had simpered and returned his glance. She looked startled and disappointed when he avoided her eyes quickly.

He had been too proud and angry to ask where Jane Grant was. And his mind would not admit that Jane and last night had anything to do with the breaking of his concentration this morning. No girl could do that to him. Not even a girl as attractive as Jane Grant.

The thought broke as he reached the small serving kitchen where he had sipped coffee with Sue Callaghan. There was relief in remembering Sue. He hesitated at the door and glanced inside. There was another nurse there preparing coffee. He stared, aware that he had stopped as the nurse sensed his presence and raised her head. The gray-green eyes widened as she saw him.

"Jane!" he gasped, coming in slowly, partially closing the door behind him. "I thought you'd transferred to the other operating room. Blake had an abdominoperineal in there—"

He stopped abruptly. He hadn't meant to say that, but the words were exactly what was in his mind. He colored. What he had said must make him sound like a jealous fool. . . .

He waited for her laughter, tensing against it, preparing to mask the words in levity, if it was not too late. But she shook her head soberly, her wide eyes troubled, as though the words were not foolish at all.

She said frankly, "When I said *that* was over, I meant it, Glen."

He was aware of the relief that was as incomprehensible as the words he had just spoken.

He forced a smile and sniffed at the coffee urn. "I could use some of that, if it's all right with the nurse in charge. I had a cup of coffee in here with Sue Callaghan one day."

"I know," she said. "I'll get you some." She turned away from him quickly.

He glanced at her covertly, wondering, as he had last night, how much Sue Callaghan *had* told her.

He said quickly, "Don't we have a dietitian on this floor?"

"Miss Cornell is off duty. She has some bug. It happens— even to dietitians who should be the healthiest of people. Sue took her job over temporarily. I was offered Sue's place on floor duties when she left. So . . ."

She glanced at him from where coffee steamed as she pulled a cup, but he seemed interested only in the stacked shelves about him.

"You're here to get away from the O.R. then?"

"If I'd been working with Dr. Blake I might have done that," she said evenly.

"You were working with me," he reminded her, almost angrily. "Not with Blake."

"I'll see you as often on the floor, Glen," she said slowly. "Didn't that occur to you?"

It hadn't. He didn't seem to be thinking clearly today.

THE DOCTOR'S PAST

But Jane was right. A number of the patients here were his —and more to come—and he would be spending plenty of time here. But—

He looked at her suspiciously. "That's right. We'll meet more often here. But I'm not conceited enough to believe that was your reason."

She looked away, so that her eyes would not tell him too plainly that it was the reason. The only reason. Here she would often be alone with him. In the wards, in here perhaps, in his office that was situated between the two main sections of the surgical service floor.

In the operating suite, she had seen him only as a masked and gowned figure, the center of a circle of assistants. She had seen him only as a pair of intense brown eyes above a mask that she had looked at with dislike because she thought he was pursuing Sue, and Sue was ... so susceptible where any good-looking man was concerned. Sue had made no secret of that. And she had been sorry for Sue Callaghan.

"Perhaps ... I got tired of the operating room," she said slowly. "Maybe that's all."

"Well!" he said awkwardly. Now that he had forced her to explain, he found suddenly that he wasn't satisfied with the explanation. A part of him had wanted her to say that he wasn't being conceited. That that was exactly why she was here.

He said, "That's a reason I can believe, at least. But I didn't come here to talk about reasons. I came in here to arrange our date, the way you promised last night. Or have you transferred away from that too?"

She looked up quickly. "You know that's not true, Glen—" She broke off abruptly. "Damn!"

"What?" Hot coffee had spilled in a saucer and he saw that it was wet and steaming slightly against the back of her hand. He was taking the cup and saucer from her at once. "Now you've burned yourself!" he said as angrily as though she was a willful child. "I'll take that. Let me see it."

"It's nothing," she said, holding her hand away from him.

"It's nothing if you like needless pain and blisters." He had produced a handkerchief and dried the back of her hand. It was already stained red, its tenderness telling her quite plainly that it was going to blister and he was right.

"Really," she protested. "It's nothing. I was careless, I guess. I looked up at you, and—"

"Which makes it my fault," he said. His eyes were searching the shelves behind her. "There should be some bicarb here...."

"It's on the second shelf," she told him resignedly. "But really, Doctor—"

He came back with it quickly and glanced at her. "You're pale."

"I'm a coward, aren't I?"

"I wouldn't say that." He mixed the solution and dabbed it on the back of her hand. "An old remedy, but useful," he said. "Takes the sting out and often stops blistering in minor burns almost at once. Against a lot of my work and teaching though, so don't advertise it."

"I won't, Doctor," she promised, smiling. She had leaned her back against the sink. Suddenly, she felt ill. Almost as though she were in shock. And the note of anxiety in his voice, she knew, was more for her pallor than the burn. She laughed. It took effort because even her lips felt bloodless, but she made it sound convincing. "As a matter of fact I haven't felt well all morning. Probably a hangover from last night."

"You had two drinks," he said. "And sat on the second for most of the night."

"Two is a lot for me," she said ruefully.

He straightened. "Hand feel better now?"

"Yes, it does." She moved her fingers experimentally. "Most of the pain is gone and the redness is fading."

She looked up and saw his anxious expression. "Really, I'm all right, Glen!" she insisted.

"You're not a good color," he said soberly, his eyes those of a doctor suddenly. Probing, questioning....

His anxiety for her filled her with a warm glow again and she was sure that her pallor was going. She said abruptly, "Good heavens! It's almost eleven, and they're waiting for these in the women's ward!" She turned quickly, putting his coffee on a fresh saucer. "I'm afraid I'm going to have to leave you here—"

"Not until we got one thing straight. Our date."

She hesitated. "I'm off duty Sunday, that leaves Saturday night free. The Midtown?"

"I'd like to take you somewhere better than that. Dinner, a later show."

THE DOCTOR'S PAST

"The others mightn't be free..." she ventured uncertainly and blushed.

"I wasn't thinking of Don Fenton and Diane. But if you want to, we'll make a foursome."

"No. It's all right."

"Just the two of us then," he said with satisfaction. "We'll have dinner and go to a show afterward. Okay?"

"Sounds wonderful," she said.

"I'll pick you up outside the nurses' residence at eight, then?"

She smiled. "We have a date, Doctor."

"Glen." He was remembering last night suddenly, the way she had felt against him when he kissed her. He felt a sudden urge to have her against him like that again right now. And her eyes told him suddenly that she wanted it too. He watched her, motionless, his eyes glowing.

"I'll have to run," she said breathlessly. Her uniform brushed against him as she reached for the tray. He smelled last night's perfume faintly and the urge to kiss her overwhelmed him.

His hands caught her as she passed, holding her without force.

"Glen, don't!" she whispered. "I'm on duty—"

"So am I."

"You'll spill the coffee!" she said in panic.

His hands turned her, feeling resistance. But her face was turned up toward him as he kissed her. Her full lips sought his then, parting before he released her. He steadied the tray.

"As a nurse you're not a very good waitress," he said. "But with you around who'd think of coffee anyway?"

"You'd be a bad influence on any waitress, Glen Carew," she said with forced lightness and walked quickly to the door, pushing the serving cart through expertly. The door closed partially behind her.

Moving the rubber-tired cart steadily along the corridor, her outward calm was not in accord with her thudding heart. The demanding pressure of his lips was still with her. She closed her eyes, fighting weakness.

"I shouldn't have let him kiss me," she thought.

But hospitals are like any other place where young men and women are thrown together in the daily round of work and living. Men and women fell in love and were loved.

"If he wants me the way it must have been with Sue," she thought, "what will I say? What will I do?"

The thought frightened her now. Because her throbbing heart, her warm body told her that she would cling to him as she had responded when he kissed her. And nothing else would matter at all.

Back in the empty serving kitchen, Glen Carew sipped his coffee perfunctorily and emptied the last half of it down the sink.

Outside he studied the length of an empty passage before he walked toward the male surgical wards, where he was already overdue for dressing rounds. He felt better now about a lot of things.

He worked smoothly in the long wards, advising, correcting minor difficulties with the charge nurse.

He worked quickly too. After he'd finished, he hurried to the women's section, where he hoped to see Jane.

"Here is Mrs. Durban, Doctor," the charge nurse said, smiling. She came round the bed with the chart and gave it to him. She motioned the duty R.N. closer with her dressing tray.

Carew skimmed the chart and smiled at his patient. "How are the arm movements coming along, Mrs. Durban?"

"I can touch my cheek now, Doctor," she said.

"Prove it then. Gently! That's right. Fine!"

"There seems some reduction of the swelling already, Doctor," the charge nurse said cheerfully.

"Sleep well last night?" he asked his patient.

"Dr. Prentice gave me sedation."

"Oh?"

He studied the chart again, aware of the charge nurse's quick interest. She said tentatively, "Dr. Prentice and Dr. Cape looked in on Mrs. Durban last night, Doctor. Miss Bradley was on duty. I talked to her at breakfast and she said they were very pleased with Mrs. Durban's progress."

"So you had visitors," he said, frowning slightly as he studied the chart. There was a rise of temperature, a quickened pulse rate, then sedation. He had ordered the sedation, but Prentice had initialed it neatly instead of the resident on call. He remembered the resident had been Victor Preedy, the most junior of the residents in the surgical service. Blake's choice. . . .

Prentice and Cape? His frown deepened.

THE DOCTOR'S PAST

"Dr. Cape told me that I was your first surgical patient here, Dr. Carew," the woman said, smiling at him. "And I told him I had every confidence in my doctor."

"That was nice of you, Mrs. Durban."

"It was the truth," she said quickly, almost defiantly. "You saved my life. Dr. Prentice said I'd have to keep on coming back for tests, but I know I'm going to be all right. And you did it. Everyone else has been wonderful, but *you* operated."

Carew smiled and handed the chart back to the nurse. "It seems I have a champion," he said. "I think we'll have the dressing off, Miss Connors."

"Yes, Doctor."

The long, S-shaped wound had granulated well. The line of skin sutures crossing it were ready to come out. The shorter axillary flap from which he had already removed the mattress sutures was closed nicely. He bent, examining the area closely. He nodded satisfaction. There seemed no contracture. He had been particularly careful in approximating the edges of the main incision exactly, and now that care was paying dividends. The scar would be very fine, which meant that the cosmetic result would be good.

He examined the still-swollen arm carefully, and straightened, smiling. If Prentice had been looking for postoperative complications here, he couldn't have found any.

And if Prentice mentioned last night's visit, then he would mention that abrupt, even though temporary fluctuation in pulse and temperature. The nursing instructions on the chart carried his notation that his patient was not to be disturbed, or excited. Quiet and bed rest were essential for her. Only her husband was allowed in as a visitor yet, because of that instruction.

Last night's visit by the chief of service and the medical superintendent had excited the patient. And it had not been any casual visit. Carew knew that. His patient must have felt it too and come instinctively, loyally to his defence.

He looked at her with affection. "We're going to take out the skin sutures this afternoon, Mrs. Durban. After that you should be able to lift your arm higher."

"So soon?" she queried, her eyes wide in the pale face. "That's wonderful."

"It's because you're such a good patient," he told her. "Dr. Cape said last night that a patient who believed in her doctor was halfway to convalescence. He *told* Dr. Prentice that. And I know he's right, because you've made me feel that way."

Cape had been on his side then. He would have liked to know what Dr. Prentice had said. But he couldn't ask. So he merely smiled at her reassuringly.

"Put a lighter dressing on, Nurse. I'll bring Dr. Wilson in after lunch and we'll remove the skin sutures. Keep it up, Mrs. Durban, you're going to walk out of here one day soon, back to your husband."

"Yes—" she smiled "—I know..."

He walked through into the Recovery Room then to have another look at his patient of the inguinal hernia.

The duty nurse in the Recovery Room smiled at him cheerfully as she handed him the chart.

"Mr. Bryant is sleeping under sedation now, Doctor. He was restless for a while. But Dr. Prentice came in to have a look at him."

"He's had sedation?"

She looked uneasy. "On Dr. Prentice's orders, Doctor."

"Bring me a stethoscope. And I want a B.P. check."

"Yes, Doctor." She hesitated. "He was *very* restless. He tried to get out of bed. We had you paged and Miss Kent looked for you in male surgical. She thought you'd be in there on dressing rounds. Then Dr. Prentice came in. He took over. He told Miss Kent you'd probably finished in the ward and gone to lunch. He said to rescind the call as he left."

"The patient needed sedation then," he said, hiding anger that was close to dismay. "But we'll check his condition now."

Prentice again! The service chief seemed intent on putting him in the wrong. Yet Prentice was right. He admitted that, reluctantly.

He had been in the serving kitchen with Jane Grant while his name had been called—and he had never heard it. And the weak fascia that he had had to suture so carefully this morning could have ruptured again but for Prentice.

He swore silently as the nurse passed him the instruments, and he began his examination.

Damn Prentice! Carew thought with unreasonable anger.

Chapter Seven

"Dr. Baker is on the staff here," Prentice explained. "Mr. Moreton is his patient. Dr. Baker has diagnosed splenic anemia. He thinks surgery is indicated—a splenectomy. We'd like you to have a look at the patient with us, Dr. Carew. He's waiting in the examination room now."

"You want me to undertake the splenectomy?" Carew asked bleakly. He had hurried from the surgical floor to one of the downstairs clinics when he had been paged and summoned there. He resented the call at once when he came in and found Prentice waiting.

"If we agree with the need for surgery," Prentice said in his careful way, "yes. I want you to take it. In that case I intend to schedule the patient for surgery tomorrow morning. With splenic anemia time is vital, as you know, Doctor."

Carew nodded. "I'm quite aware of the importance of the time factor, Dr. Prentice."

He expected a short retort from his service chief. His lips thinned, but the older man merely nodded. "We'll go in at once," Prentice said calmly. "We'll examine the patient together."

Following him into the examination room, Carew scowled at the alert, briskly walking figure of the chief of the surgical service. Even when Prentice angered him most, he could never quite dislike him. Perhaps that was because he was becoming increasingly aware that Dr. Prentice's probing study of his new surgeon held no personal malice.

Prentice was doing his job as chief of the surgical service with the cold precision of a surgical instrument. And if Carew was not the man that Prentice wanted here at Midtown, he suspected that Prentice would dispense with him as coldly as he would excise a diseased organ from one of his patients. Prentice was a perfectionist.

Carew wondered what Prentice was like beneath that professional exterior. It occurred to him suddenly that he had made no attempt to find out.

He watched the burly Dr. Baker straighten beside the patient on the examination table as the two surgeons came in. Baker was as tall but broader than Carew, with a shock of graying hair and strong bifocals that made his eyes look abnormally large. He had a strong face, and was, Carew knew, a specialist of high repute in the diagnosis and treatment of diseases of the blood.

"This is Dr. Carew, Doctor," Prentice said in his calm voice. "In case you haven't met?"

Baker nodded. "Hello, Doctor. I think we shared a meal one day in the dining room. With Dr. Fenton." He picked up the case history from its clip and skimmed through it quickly. "Mr. Moreton is not only a patient of mine—he's an old friend. No need for any secrecy. He knows what's the matter with him as well as I do. And he's prepared for surgery, if we agree that he's going to benefit by it."

"Started vomiting blood a couple of years ago," the patient said with forced cheerfulness. His eyes expressed the anxiety that his voice hid as he looked at Carew.

Carew smiled at him. In war he had seen that look in men's eyes—that instinctive rebellion against what they'd been told was fact, always hoping that another opinion might prove the first one wrong.

"It's a typical clinical picture of splenic anemia," Baker said. "Chronic, so we have to do something about it. And since medicine can't stop its progress we may have to use surgery. It started insidiously. The hematemesis that Mr. Moreton mentioned was a fairly early symptom. It made the diagnosis possible. The spleen is enlarged and hard. Feel it, Carew. Reaches damned near down to his umbilicus! The hematemesis has become recurrent—he vomits blood fre-

THE DOCTOR'S PAST

quently now. The liver is slightly enlarged at this stage of the disease. There's jaundice, as you can see from his color."

Carew's long fingers probed; he straightened, Prentice palpated then, frowning, precise.

"Mr. Moreton has had pathological tests?" Prentice asked.

"They're here," Baker grunted. "Anemia of a microcytic type, with a low color index and a leukopenia. A very low count."

Carew said, "What about the anemic symptoms?"

"Breathlessness, palpitation, lassitude, and pallor. We've steadied it down a little. Mr. Moreton is as ready for surgery as he can be."

"We'll check his general condition," Prentice said. "I'd like to see the latest pathological report, X-rays. . . ."

Carew started the physical examination. It was better than he hoped. The case history said that the patient was forty. He looked a lot older than that. Nearer sixty. There was emaciation. The pulse was fast and thready. Pressure low.

The patient's strength was failing and would surely decline rapidly now. But there *was* still strength, resistance, in the skinny body. He would never again be as ready for major surgery, for a splenectomy, as he was today.

Carew came back to the others. "I believe he can stand surgery very well, if it's indicated."

Baker grinned at his patient. "Hear that, Jim? Got plenty of strength. Well, we'll see if we agree on surgery. I have some X-rays in the other room." He nodded at his patient reassuringly. "Pull up the covers, Jim. I'll be right back."

He ushered them out into the clinic office. He put the case history down on the desk and looked at them.

"Well?"

"I agree with the diagnosis," Prentice said. "Carew, you examined his physical condition?"

"That was the only question in my mind," Carew said. "I think he can surely stand the operation. And as long as that's true, there's not the slightest objection to it. As you know, the results of a splenectomy for this kind of thing are usually dramatically successful—and even if they weren't, I'd be in favor of it. After all, one can spare a spleen better than most other organs, without any ill effect. And here its removal is most definitely indicated."

Baker had been scrutinizing Carew carefully as he spoke.

He nodded, as if satisfied with what he'd heard, and said, "In that case..."

"Dr. Carew will take him in the morning at ten," Prentice said. "And he will look after the preoperative preparation, of course. You'd prefer that, wouldn't you, Dr. Carew?"

The addition had made it sound a little more human. Carew swallowed his indignation and returned Baker's smile. "Yes, of course. He'll need transfusion, Doctor. Do we have his group?"

"I'll look after that and the admission," Baker said. "He's had large doses of iron which should help." He started to gather his papers. "I have clinic at four. I'd like to talk to you about him, Dr. Carew, and be there when you're preparing him if that's possible."

Carew nodded. "Be on the surgical floor around five, Doctor."

"Thanks," Baker said. He glanced from one to the other of them briefly. "A man should send his friends to another doctor," he said. "Treating someone you like when they're really ill is like delivering your own wife, dammit."

Carew followed Prentice out into the passage again. Prentice slowed, waiting for him.

"You must have performed a great many splenectomies in army surgery, Doctor, of course."

Carew said carefully. "Mostly ruptured."

"You may find this one a little different."

"It's enlarged. It isn't torn, ruptured, cut open. It's whole. And large enough to grasp," Carew said coldly. "In surgery of the spleen a knowledge of the anatomy of the nearby organs and their identification is the greatest essential. Adequate exposure and careful dissection come within normal surgical ability, which I believe I have or I wouldn't be practicing. I don't need to study the anatomy, Doctor, if that's what you had in mind!"

"Did I say that?" Prentice raised his eyebrows. His calm eyes judged Glen Carew briefly. "I think not. I was about to remind you, however, that this case could be different from those you've known. If I were the surgeon, I'd be thinking about the possibility of dense adhesions caused by perisplenitis. Adhesions containing blood vessels, inflamed, binding the spleen to neighboring tissues, organs, vessels. Perisplenitis can make surgery of the spleen very difficult when the case is anemic. Tear an adhesion and you have a

THE DOCTOR'S PAST

hermorrhage. I don't have to tell you that the man back there can't afford to lose blood."

Carew stopped, angrily, to stare at him.

"Why not say what you really mean, Doctor? You watched the inguinal hernia reduction. Saw me fumble through a Farris technique I didn't expect. You thought I took too long with the operation."

"If you'd been more familiar with the Farris technique you would certainly have been quicker," Prentice said with the same calm.

"You thought I should've stayed in the residence the night before to read up on the Farris?" Carew demanded angrily.

"I hoped you would, Dr. Carew."

"If you wanted me to do that, why the hell didn't you make it an order?"

Momentarily, Carew saw the beginning of anger in Prentice's eyes so that their light brown seemed tawny. It faded.

He said quietly, "I didn't make it an order Dr. Carew, because this is not the army. This is a hospital. We work as individuals here, subject to supervision, but not a harsh supervision. Here, we expect our resident surgeons to work things like that out for themselves."

"Do you? You checked the patient afterward in the Recovery Room. You seem to have the habit of checking my patients after surgery. Did you find anything wrong? Were you dissatisfied with the patient's condition?"

"No."

"All right," Carew said. "I'll see that you're not, Doctor! And when I see the need for study, I'll study. But when I'm not on call, what I do is my own damned business!"

He stared at Prentice, shipping his anger—hoping for an outburst as angry as his own had been, so that he could sustain it.

Prentice remained calm. "I've never doubted your ability as a surgeon, Dr. Carew. You proved that before you came here."

"Then what do you doubt?" Carew's face was flushed.

For the first time Prentice frowned. "Do you still remember med school, Carew? Internship?—your early days as a doctor? I do. I wasn't brilliant, and it took effort to study. Great effort. You had to learn it all, each phrase, each page, each chapter of each textbook to get through, to graduate. Hundreds of pages to each book, and scores of books.

And when you got through, when you'd learned it all, you found that while you'd been learning they'd discovered new techniques, new processes. You had to start to learn all over again. And when you'd learned the new things, there were more new things discovered while you learned. You found there was no end to it. That hasn't changed, Carew. There's still no end to it. Not even if you specialize and stick to one subject. That narrows the field certainly, but you've still got to keep up. You must have found that out in the army. You discovered new techniques, perfected others in reconstructive work yourself."

"So?"

"So, suddenly, you've entered a wider field, Carew. General surgery. One of the widest fields. Do you really think you know it all?"

"Is that what's the matter with you?" Carew asked. "You think I haven't kept up?"

"The Farris technique, Carew," Prentice said gently. He turned and walked away.

"Son of a bitch!" Carew whispered between his teeth. He stifled an impulse to hurry after Prentice's slowly walking figure. Blazing with anger, he turned back toward the wards.

His fury carried him past the elevators and he walked on into his own office and closed the door hard. He lit a cigarette, but he couldn't smoke it. He went out into the wards again, forcing himself to calm, finding relief of anger only in the release of energy as he worked.

Later, hours later, walking down the steps of the hospital with Dr. Baker, a part of his mind was still listening to Stanley Prentice, even as they discussed the patient for tomorrow morning's surgery.

Baker at least had confidence in him. He was saying as he climbed into his car, "Well, I'm glad he's *your* patient tomorrow, Dr. Carew. I don't know anyone I'd sooner have do the job. That's one of the penalties of treating someone you know as well as I know Jim Moreton. You share it with them. You suffer too. We've golfed together and sat over a Scotch. Our wives visit. But now he's in your hands and I feel a lot better about it. I'll not observe in the morning. No with Jim. But I'd like you to call me afterward. Would yo mind?"

"Glad to, Doctor," Carew said.

He glanced up at the windows of the hospital as the ca

pulled away. He wished Prentice could have heard that. He turned back to find Baker's gloved hand raised in salute as the car went through the gates.

He thrust his hands into his pockets and hurried across the parking area toward the residence. His anger at Prentice came back slowly. It mounted as he ran up the stairs to his first floor quarters, not bothering to wait for the elevator. He needed a drink, something to break the tension. He looked at his fingers, they were trembling.

Prentice had not only angered him. There was worry also. Because there had been truth in what Prentice had said. Too much damned truth. He found a bottle of Scotch and poured a drink quickly. What did Prentice expect a man to be? A damned automaton?

He partly emptied the glass. What he needed tonight was company, so he opened his door again and looked down the passage. Fenton's door was closed and there was no light beneath it. He looked toward the lounge and could see men in there sprawled in the comfortable chairs. A television flickered in a darkened room. He decided against that.

He closed his door, finished the drink and poured another. That was another thing that Prentice could have mentioned, Carew decided as he stared moodily at the amber liquor. He *was* trying to play a little, to have fun here at Midtown. But all the same....

He chose a textbook from the shelves and sat down with the whisky. He opened the book on his knees and flipped the pages.

"Operations on the spleen and portal hypertension...."

"The first essential for splenic surgery is adequate exposure," he read. He read slowly, sipping the Scotch.

"... dense adhesions from perisplenitis may make splenectomy very difficult in these cases...."

He hurled the textbook into a corner. "Stay there, goddamn you!" he almost snarled at it. "I'm going out!"

He stalked into the bedroom and picked up the phone on the bedside table. He flipped the single digit that gave him the switchboard.

"Dr. Carew here. Can you get me Miss Grant in the nurses' residence?"

"Yes, Doctor."

He waited impatiently, his anger receding, however, as he thought of Jane.

"I'm sorry, Doctor," the smooth voice of the operator said. "Miss Grant isn't answering. I can put the call through to the house mother, if you like?"

He thought about that briefly. "There must be some other way to contact her?"

"Is it a personal call, Doctor?" Her voice had a sympathetic tone.

Carew said gruffly, "Yes, it is."

"I'll try the lounge," she said quickly. "One of the girls in there will find her. Hold the line."

"Thank you," he said, in relief.

"Hello?" a girlish voice said abruptly, ushered in by a burst of music low in the background. "This is Miss Brereton speaking."

"I'd like to speak to Miss Grant," he said. "She isn't in her room. Do you think you could find her for me, Miss Brereton?"

"Uh-huh," she said. "I'll try. Who is calling?"

"Santa Claus," he said.

She giggled. "Jane was in here earlier. But she doesn't seem to be around. I'll ask Diane Foster—they're friends. Hold the line, Santa."

He felt better. Then Diane's voice came on the line from a background of laughter, "Who *is* that?"

"I just told Miss Brereton," Carew chuckled with her.

"Oh!" she said. "It's *you!*"

"Uh-huh! Where's Jane, Diane? I've just had one of those days. Someone walked over my grave. I've had it. The only therapy is to go out and have a time."

"*I'm* not doing anything," she said. But her voice had changed subtly, become wary.

"I'm flattered, Diane! Thanks. But Don mightn't like it. And I want to speak to Jane. Can you find her for me? Please?"

"I was kidding, of course."

"I know. Is she there?"

"No."

"Where is she? We had a date tomorrow night. But I don't want to wait that long. I want to talk to her tonight. Even if it's only for a few minutes."

"Are you serious?"

"Yes."

The phone was silent a moment before she said quietly, "Jane went out."

There was a surprised silence. Then he said with forced lightness, "Well—our date wasn't for tonight. Thanks—"

"Wait," she said. "It isn't quite the way you think."

"What do you mean?"

"Well... Jane and I have been pretty close since Sue left."

"I know that."

"She... likes you," Diane said. She hesitated. Her next words were abrupt. "She's gone to the Midtown." She lowered her voice. "She went there to meet Paul. You know about that don't you? She went to tell him that... Glen! Glen, are you there?"

But he hadn't heard any of her explanation. He had jammed the phone back on its cradle furiously. He was already out in the other room pouring a drink. It did him no good. Tonight, today, nothing was any good—everything was wrong. And the feeling crawled over him that it could get worse. That it wasn't ended yet.

"She's gone to the Midtown. She went there to meet Paul...."

"Goddam it!" he thought viciously. "She *said* that was ended. She told me it was and I believed her. Yet Blake only has to whistle for her to come running!"

The anger growing within him all day swelled abruptly. So that was how they treated you here. You couldn't trust anyone, except yourself—or maybe a patient who thought she owed you her life. All the rest were against you. You couldn't even trust the girl you thought was halfway in love with you.

"Okay!" he said aloud. "Okay...."

He could do without them all. And he would. What was he doing here, anyway? Back there across the Pacific, at least *Colonel* Carew had been among friends. Working with men like himself. Patients who at least had a common interest. Made into a pattern by discipline, war....

He poured another drink and looked at the empty bottle. Drinking was a phony release from tension. You felt worse afterward. A lot worse. But right now it was what he needed, and the bottle was empty.

He remembered patients who had shaken his hand and thanked him. He had treated some of them against their will, because they *wanted* to die. And he'd made them whole, watched hope come, then gratitude. He'd seen them walk away to the new life he had made for them. And that had been the one good thing in the seemingly never-ending drudgery.

Suddenly now, he wanted the company of such men again. He couldn't find it here. Not even with Don Fenton. The men he'd treated had come from other walks of life. He thought of Fred Champion over at the Midtown Bar and his two ex-marine helpers...

He was past the lounge and halfway down the stairs before he noticed that he was still in his hospital coat.

In the Midtown Bar, Jane Grant was staring angrily at the man across the table, an untasted drink before her. Paul Blake glared back at her sullenly, running his fingers through thick, curly black hair with an exasperated gesture.

"Okay!" he muttered. His light brown, almost amber eyes avoided hers suddenly. "Okay! So Sue told you that. But that girl couldn't lie in bed straight. She was jealous, and she lied. I was taking *you* out. Don't you understand how Sue felt about that? Look, Jane—"

"No!" she said.

"She lied!" he almost shouted at her. "And the way you've been talking, Jane, anyone would think I *seduced* her." He laughed. "God! You don't know Sue. You just *don't* know her."

"I know you, Paul," she said. *"Now."* She stood up. "Good-bye."

"Shh!" he said in a low voice and glanced around uneasily. "It'll be all over the hospital in the morning that we quarreled."

"We haven't quarreled," she said. "We're just through."

"Have I hurt *you?*" he demanded.

"I don't intend to give you the chance."

"Look," he said. "I'll take you back to the hospital now. We'll talk about it tomorrow when you've cooled down. A girl like that! A man should make her prove the things she says. She was never any good." He allowed anger to enter his voice openly. "And you'd let a no-good like her break up what's between us."

"There's nothing between us, Paul."

"Okay," he said furiously. "Maybe you're entitled to bitch

THE DOCTOR'S PAST

a little. Of course I laid Sue. Everyone did. She was just a tramp. You don't have to be jealous about her. Jane, wait!"

He stood up angrily with her. But she had slipped out from the seat and was walking stiffly toward the door. Blake stared after her uncertainly, red-faced, aware that they had attracted the attention of a group of interns and nurses at another table.

He cursed and sat down again. If she felt that way—he didn't have to run after her. But they were laughing openly at the other table now, their laughter only fading as he changed his mind and stood up again. He stared in memorizing each laughing face deliberately, before he walked toward the bar. The laughter of the interns faded abruptly. Most of them disliked him. He knew that. But he knew also that they were all a little frightened of him. Any resident who disliked an intern in his service could make it tough for the intern. Could make him wish he'd never been born.

They turned back quickly to their drinks again, pretending they hadn't noticed him. Blake grunted and walked on.

He threw a bill on the bar and walked outside and stared about angrily. Jane Grant was gone.

Furious, she had hurried down the long room. But there had been fear mixed with her anger too, so that she almost collided with Pete, the waiter, as he skillfully whisked a tray of glasses out of her way. His surprised glance changed as he looked at her.

"Are you all right, Miss?"

"I'm sorry!" She walked on more quickly. In the brief encounter, she had seen Blake getting up again. Momentarily as she turned, she knew panic, expecting to feel his hand on her arm.

Pete called after her, "Miss! You want me to get you a cab?"

But she had forgotten Pete as she ran the steps. As she ran across the street. She glanced back and saw Blake coming out the door, his head turning as he looked for her. She ran into the shadows of the nearest alley.

She was fifty yards down the alley before she realized that it was unlighted and lonely, that she should not be here. The hospital staff always walked around the block when they came to the Midtown Bar, avoiding the intersecting lanes and the often blind alleys that crossed them. But

Blake was back there outside the Midtown and she had no intention of going back.

The thoroughfare she had entered was narrow, with no sidewalks. It was unlighted, with blank, windowless, high walls of warehouses stretching away to a spot of light that she knew was the street that paralleled the one behind her. The distant street ahead was well lighted and she could see cars passing the end of the lane, and an occasional pedestrian.

There was safety in the very darkness of this lane, she decided. It was like a gun aimed at the light down there, with herself looking down the empty barrel. She would have felt more nervous, she told herself firmly, if this place *had* been lighted, as were the alleys where the tenements stood farther along.

She might have had something to be frightened about there. In those crude dwellings lived a cross section of humanity that she had seen often enough in the Emergency Room of big city hospitals, beaten, stabbed, kicked. Or addicted.... There adolescent gangs prowled, fighting over girls, robbing the unwary with violence. The lower strata of criminal society lived there too. Pimps, prostitutes, petty criminals. Violent men and evil women....

She pushed the frightening thoughts away and walked on more rapidly, her footsteps sounding sharp in the narrow lane between its high walls. She was a nurse, and nurses weren't supposed to be frightened. Even people like that respected a nurse.

Ahead of her abruptly, the lane opened on either side into blind alleys that gave access to loading docks behind the buildings on either side; she heard the subdued murmur of men's voices.

She was afraid suddenly, the fear weakening her knees, making her stomach churn, although she could see nobody in there. There was a light, but it was only a weak globe with a white shield over one of the closed and padlocked loading docks.

She walked softly, warily, knowing sickly that if anyone had been listening, her footsteps would have been heard a hundred yards back. If anyone here meant to harm her it was too late for caution.

The voices had stopped abruptly as she passed the docks. Suddenly, there was movement behind her. She heard the

THE DOCTOR'S PAST

swift pad of feet in rubber-soled shoes coming after her. She started to run. And as she ran, with her heart thumping she saw the doorway ahead on her left and a figure starting out of it to stop her.

She veered away, but he was too fast. He ran beside her momentarily, before he grasped her left arm, dragging at it, slowing and stopping her as she turned furiously upon him. He seemed little more than a boy. He was lighter than she was, and he was having difficulty in holding her arm as she tried to wrench away from him. She swung her handbag and hit at his face with it. Her arm wrenched free as he cried out.

Then someone else caught her right arm and the strap of her bag broke. She lost it. Struggling, she felt her left arm grasped. There were three of them now, hustling her back against the wall near the corner.

"She hit me!" one of them snarled. "She shun't 'a hit me like that, the bitch!"

"Where d'you think you're going, beautiful?" the one holding her right arm demanded, pushing her back hard against the wall. He was breathing heavily, as though he'd run a long way, although they'd only had to chase her a few yards, and he was bigger than the other two.

"You ain't frightened of us, are ya?" the one holding her left arm said.

"What you hit me for, eh?" the third whined, his hand against his face.

"I'm a nurse," she said. The words sounded calm, but that wasn't the way she felt. It was as though the voice didn't belong to her. "I'm going back to Midtown Hospital."

There was a crude laugh.

"She's a nurse, she says."

"Where's your uniform, Nurse?" another sneered.

"Take a look in her bag, Benny," the biggest of them said. "Maybe she keeps it in there."

He was stronger than either of the others and he leaned against her, pinning her to the wall. She could feel his excitement, smell their unwashed bodies sickeningly with senses that seemed sharpened by fear.

"Ain't got a uniform," the boy she'd hit said, searching her bag. "But she's got a fist fulla bills...." He stuffed them in his pocket. "Let's get outa here!"

"You can keep the money," her voice said. "But you must

let me go. I have to go back to the hospital. I'm a nurse—"

"Come on," the boy called Benny said. *"Come on!"*

The biggest boy leaned against her harder. He had her arm against the wall, and the concrete was hurting her arm and her back. She tried to kick him and he hit her face with his open hand. Not hard, but the blow seemed to leave him breathless.

"She hit *you*, Benny," he panted. "Don't you want to get even?"

"No!" Benny said. "Let her go. We got her money."

"Aw, come on, Benny! Let's rough her up a bit! Come on!" He was pulling her toward the corner only a few yards back, and the other boy, still gripping her left arm, was working her back along the wall with sharp pushes, overbalancing her with each thrust, so that the corner came closer steadily, sidelong, and the faint light above the docks.

"Let's have a look at her," the boy holding her left arm said. "Most nurses is finks, anyway. Not worth sacking with."

"Not this one," the biggest said. "She feels different. . . ."

She could see them now. Dark-haired, patterned almost like brothers. Latin, with pale faces and eyes that seemed black. Blue-gray jeans with metal studs, dirty black shirts. Benny might have been fourteen or fifteen. The others older, their eyes more evil. Thin, sallow, ignorant, old beyond their years. . . .

She was fighting desperately suddenly and there was no longer any pretense. A leg locked around hers, tripping her. She fell. They dragged her into the alley near the docks. She screamed and a dirty hand clapped over her mouth. She bit it, fighting back as one of them hit her again. She screamed.

Suddenly there were other feet pounding and Benny was yelling in a high, shrill voice.

"Look out! Look out! Look out!"

Violent movement surged about her as she tried dazedly to get up. She glimpsed a figure in white, heard yells, the thump of quick blows. The boy Benny ran back into the lane and was gone, his whimpering cries receding rapidly. The one who had held her left arm tripped over her. He rolled away to come up and was knocked down again. He crawled toward the corner where he got up unsteadily, bleeding, and ran after Benny.

But the third, the biggest, wasn't getting away. The man

THE DOCTOR'S PAST

in the white coat, who she realized now was Glen Carew, had him backed in the far corner near the docks. Carew's tall figure moved from side to side, blocking escape as the bully tried to dodge away.

She heard a shrill, frightened yell. Something metallic clattered near her as it was tossed away, fell and spun, slowing, its switchblade reflecting the light. She got up, unsteadily, and leaned against the wall, wanting to retch, but putting her foot on the knife because she felt too sick to bend and pick it up or throw it away.

Through the haze enveloping her, she heard the frightened, gasping cry again, the quick flurry of shuffling feet. Blows. . . .

There was silence then, and Carew was coming back to her, tall, his face white as he gripped her shoulders and looked at her.

"Are you all right?" he demanded.

"Yes. I'm fine. He ... didn't really hurt me." It was her voice speaking, without any conscious command from her mind. Her hands were adjusting her clothing automatically, pulling down the warm sweater over the broken straps of her bra and her small rounded breasts.

"You're sure?"

"Yes."

"Want me to bring him along to the police?"

"No," her voice said. "You came along before they ... really harmed me. I just want to get out of here."

"Come on then!" he said gruffly. He took her arm, almost as fiercely as that other hand had seized it.

"You haven't ... hurt him badly?"

"I should've killed the sonsofbitches—all of them! But the little one ran too fast. The others are just beaten up. They'll get home. This one might have to crawl—but he'll get there, damn him!"

Her body was trembling and his grip was hurting her arm. Her legs started walking. They turned the corner back into the empty lane. Her legs walked uncertainly, taking her toward the light.

"Goddam it!" he said gruffly. "Where was Blake? *Where the hell was he?* They could've killed you!"

"Blake?" her voice said almost curiously.

"You went to the Midtown Bar with him, didn't you? *Well, didn't you? After* you'd told me you weren't going to see him again?" He scowled. It seemed to her almost as if he wanted to find Blake and beat the suave, sophisticated resident up too. Violence in him that she had never suspected before showed nakedly in his eyes, in his breathing.

Her mind, which seemed outside herself, observing, thought with satisfaction, "He'd like to beat Paul up too. For good measure. Not because he loves me—but because something inside him released when he hit those boys. So he'd beat Paul too. And the funny thing is—I'd like him to do it."

"Well?" he demanded.

"Well, what?" her voice said calmly.

"Where was Blake? And what the hell were you doing walking through this lane?"

"I left the Midtown before Paul. He didn't come with me. Why should he? I'd just told him we were through, that I never intended to go out with him again. I tried to tell him over the phone, but he wouldn't listen. So we met at the Midtown instead. It made no difference to what I meant to say to him. He thought it would—but he knows better now."

He stopped her abruptly.

"That was why you went to the Midtown?"

"Did you think there was another reason?"

He was holding her still, and she could hear the thump of his heart as he stared down at her—or perhaps that was her own heart she could hear. His hands holding her trembled.

"I thought you'd decided that you and Blake...God!" he muttered thickly. He held her against him suddenly, so tightly that she breathed with difficulty. *"It tore me apart!"* he said in agony.

"Why?"

"You know why," he said. "Because I was crazy jealous."

"Jealous?"

His hands moved, stroking her hair, her back, molding her woman's shape out of the darkness within the lane. As though he wanted to make sure that she was whole, and his....

"God!" he said. "When I turned the corner and saw that it was you they had in there! I love you, Jane—don't you know that?"

These were the words her mind had waited to hear. And now, satisfied, her mind seemed to be letting go. It was no longer standing beside her, observing. It was floating into darkness and oblivion, leaving her body drooping, supported only by his arms. She could not tell him all the things she wanted to say. About the way she felt. About loving him.

He was calling her name, anxiously, but the sound faded and was lost. . . .

Chapter Eight

"Retractors."

Glen Carew watched the red abdominal incision widen as the blunt retractors took hold. Tom Linton had drawn the muscle and fascia back almost to the cage of the ribs, and on the other side, a nervous Jeff Wilson was drawing the abdominal wall on that side back carefully over the stomach and omentum.

The subcostal incision was giving him quite good exposure now, but he had shrunk the swollen spleen by preoperative injections of epinephrine. And he had ligated the splenic artery to shrink it still farther, and return as much blood from the spleen as possible back into the circulation.

Now he was faced with the task of removing a spleen that had shrunk back beneath the cage of ribs. And the spleen in there, he knew now, had many adhesions. To deliver it into the wound that he had made, he must clear it by the use of his fingers, the sense of touch; he could not see it.

"Pulse and pressure?"

"Pulse is very weak," the anesthetist said. "B.P. and temperature falling. I'm finding it hard to get a diastolic pressure now."

Glen Carew listened to the readings. He nodded. His eyes checked the steady drip of the transfusion that was keeping

THE DOCTOR'S PAST

Dr. Baker's patient, Jim Moreton, alive. Only you must not think of your patient as a person. That had been his trouble last night when he had helped Jane into the Emergency Room.

He forced that thought away. Frowning, he eased his long fingers into the wound, reaching up beneath the ribs, feeling for the first band of adhesion, starting to clear it gently with his fingers. He worked slowly, carefully, his hand easing farther into the wound; his fingers curving around the organ checked and double-checked. He found an adhesion that he couldn't clear. Too dense. He was forced to divide and clamp it by sense of touch. But gradually, his fingers cleared the organ of adhesions and reached back toward the posterior parietal peritoneum attachment, the membrane joining the back of the spleen to the wall of the cavity. He had his hand in the abdomen now to the wrist.

He cleared it slowly, and straightened, gesturing to his forehead. Turning his head aside. His eyes sought the clock. At least Prentice would not be able to say that he was taking too long with the splenectomy.

If Prentice came in . . .

He bent again as the circulating nurse walked away with her towel. He tried not to think about another girl he had seen do that.

He was delivering the organ into the incision now. It cleared slowly.

"Gauze pack, Dr. Wilson."

The intern slid a heavy gauze pad moistened in normal saline solution beneath the spleen and placed it in the now empty bed to control oozing from the adhesions, and to keep the organ from slipping back in.

Carew worked on. He started identifying the vessels in the pedicle, separating them

He was working well today, and knew it. Yet this was one day when he should be nervous, edgy, lacking concentration. At the back of his mind all the time was the echo of last night's anxiety. When he had closed his eyes in concentration as he groped for adhesions about the spleen, he had seen Jane's face as she had looked last night in the Emergency Room. Her face had the pallor of death. He kept remembering now that he had seen her pale like that before.

"I'm afraid I'm a coward," she had said, trying to smile. That had been when she burned herself in the diet kitchen.

Shock could explain what had happened last night. But shock did not quite account for the other pallor. And last night in Emergency?

He had separated the pedicle stalk of the spleen from the tail of the pancreas. He started placing curved clamps around the pedicle.

He had expected to find Linton or Preedy in the Emergency Room with an intern or two assisting. But it had been a frowning Prentice who had examined Jane with him, had revived her.

Concussion, he had thought when he brought her in. He had kept telling himself that she must have hit her head when they threw her down. And slight concussion was not so bad.

He hadn't been thinking clearly. It hadn't been concussion. It should have been obvious that it was not. Prentice had disproved that quickly. There was no superficial injury consistent with concussion. The symptoms conflicted.

But there had been enough bruising on Jane Grant's perfect body to bring probing questions from an angry Prentice when he found them. And in the end, before Jane had regained consciousness, he had had to tell Prentice what had happened in self-defense.

"Show me your hands, Carew!" Prentice had ordered, then examined them. "Can you operate tomorrow?"

"Of course. They're not skinned."

"There's swelling and stiffness," Prentice had said. But he had nodded, frowning, "Very well. Operate, unless they're worse in the morning. Call me if your hand is too stiff. I'll have someone else take the splenectomy."

And then he had said something that surprised Carew. "She's lovely, isn't she, even looking like death? And you like her."

"I . . . love her."

Prentice had nodded again, without looking up from his study of the girl. "These bruises are consistent with a fall," he had said slowly. "And so far as anyone else knows—that is exactly what happened tonight, Dr. Carew. Nothing else."

Carew cut through the pedicle between the two clamps nearest to the spleen. The spleen still held in the other clamp dropped into the waiting receptacle. He let his breath sigh out and watched Tom Linton sponge the area clear of the red ooze of blood. His mind returned to last night. . . .

THE DOCTOR'S PAST

"There's no superficial injury here to indicate concussion," Prentice had said. "Some mild fever. A few points under the hundred so far. But it isn't falling. It's steady. There was fairly deep coma, pallor.... I'm not going to make a tentative diagnosis. But I'll tell you what I am going to do, Miss Grant—I'm going to call the nursing office and see that you're relieved of all duties until you have a check-up. I'm going to make an appointment with Dr. Jackson for you in the morning. I'll have him check to see whether you're well enough to come over here, or whether he sees you in the infirmary in the nurses' residence."

He'd looked at Carew then, as he said, "Jackson is a very good physician."

Carew moved in as Linton stepped back.

"Ligature."

The heavy, chromic catgut ligature came into his hand and he passed it around the stump of the pedicle close to the remaining clamp. As he tightened the ligature, Linton removed the clamp slowly, so that the ligature slid easily around the crushed portion where the clamp had gripped.

He removed the remaining clamp and nodded to Jeff Wilson. The intern took away the reddened gauze packing. Linton sponged.

Glen Carew remembered walking back to the hospital after he had left Jane with a disturbed house mother. And in the Emergency Room, Prentice had looked up from a pile of admission slips as though he expected him to come back.

"Well?" Carew had asked, frowning. He had never seen Dr. Prentice look like that before. Tired... almost old.

"It could be any one of a number of mild pyrexial infections."

"Or shock."

"Yes. Severe emotional shock could do it."

"Except that she's a trained nurse. Emergencies aren't new to her."

"That kind of personal emergency is."

"Anything else would be a coincidence. I mean, happening in conjunction with what she went through tonight."

He remembered how Prentice had nodded. Then Prentice had said, "It will occur to you later, as it has to me, that it could also be some form of anemia." He held up a hand quickly. "Don't forget that there are a number of forms of anemia. Not all devastating, Carew. And some of them are fairly prevalent among young women of her age. Jackson will start checking tomorrow and Jackson knows his business."

"Pathology—" he started to say, shocked and protesting.

"Full blood count. A test meal and a van den Bergh reaction test. Jackson will pass her on to Baker if there's any doubt at all—for further tests."

"There can't be anything like that," he had said, remembering Baker's specialty. "No!"

Glen Carew watched the operative area clear beneath Linton's careful sponging. The anesthetist called the readings of pulse, pressure, and respiration in a low voice.

Carew bent, searching the upper left abdomen for bleeding points. He found several at once that must be controlled, either by ligature or electrocautery. Brusquely he ordered Wilson to move the electrocautery unit in closer. He went to work.

He tied off the last bleeder, made the last careful search for accessory spleens. The closure began. He started placing deep sutures.

Skin sutures came into his hand as he glanced up at the clock. He started sweating suddenly and had to stop. The heat of the O.R. had nothing to do with that sweating, he knew. Over in the nurses' residence Dr. Jackson was now examining Jane. Perhaps a blood sample, other samples, were already being taken to Pathology for tests.

Too much was happening for him to realize that last night, for the first time, he had seen Dr. Stanley Prentice as a man.

The incision closed. The dressing covered the thin line of the closed incision, with the skin sutures like the rungs of a ladder crossing it. He gave the immediate postoperative instructions for Recovery Room treatment, and tore off his mask. He had never cleaned up as perfunctorily after a major operation. He answered Wilson's questions in curt monosyllables, so that the intern gave up and turned to a grinning Tom Linton.

He was halfway down the passage, still buttoning his hospital coat, when he remembered his promise to Baker. He cursed and found a phone to make the call in one of the nurses' stations. He ran across the parking area in cold air that the weak November sun could not warm.

Only in the nurses' home he must not run, he must observe decorum, protocol. To the house mother he was a doc-

THE DOCTOR'S PAST

tor interested in a patient he had brought in after a fall last night.

So he walked with the house mother sedately. He fenced with her curiosity. She took him into the small infirmary, and waited ostentatiously in the background for a few moments before she left them alone.

Glen Carew looked at the girl sitting up in the plain hospital bed in a frilly nightgown and bed jacket. Right now he could not look at her as a doctor. There was color in her cheeks, increasing as he looked at her. The slightly lemon pallor of last night was completely gone, except for slight shading beneath her eyes.

"Now I can talk to you," he said.

"She'll be back," she warned him, smiling.

"What did Jackson say?"

Her eyes avoided his, but her smile held. "He ... took some samples for Pathology. He believes I could be anemic."

"He can't be sure," he said.

"Not until tomorrow when he gets the Path. report. There's nothing to worry about, of course."

He smiled. "Of course not. Anemia!" he added disparagingly.

"With modern treatment," she said, "it's not as serious."

"Exactly."

"He's inclined to think it's the Plummer-Vinson syndrome. Iron deficiency. So if it's just dietary ..." She laughed.

"Iron for you," he said. "And Vitamin B."

"I asked him about tonight. Whether I had to stay in the infirmary—"

"Hey, wait a minute!" he said. He picked up her wrist, his fingers finding her pulse. He looked at his watch, frowning.

"Pulse fast," she said.

"How did you know?"

She smiled. "You're holding my wrist, Doctor. B.P. slightly raised. Respiration fast. Color high."

He put her wrist down gently, studying her. "Do you mean that, Jane?"

She said a little breathlessly, "It makes me feel that way. Why?"

"Last night in the lane, just before you passed out, we talked. I've been wondering all morning if you remembered."

She was no longer smiling. Her eyes watching him seemed

darker, but they held his, warming, starting to glow with a look that Glen Carew had never seen in a woman's eyes before.

"I think I was trying to hang on, to—to make you say what you said. Yes, I remember, Glen."

"I . . . said I loved you."

"I know."

He was confused. "I wasn't sure you heard. You . . . started to pass out. You didn't answer. I thought at first that you'd just fainted, emotional strain from what happened before. I tried to revive you. I carried you to the street, and called a cab—"

"Glen!" Her voice stopped him.

"Yes?"

"I wanted to answer you last night. There were a lot of things I wanted to say. I'll say them tonight, if you meant what you said then. Did you?"

"Yes, I did," he declared firmly. "But right now, you're ill. With anemia—you know you should rest."

"We have a date tonight. Remember? Dr. Jackson said I could get up. I'm relieved of all duties until the report comes back from Pathology. But I'm not confined to bed, or the hospital. At least not until his diagnosis is verified by Pathology—if it is."

He frowned. "How do you feel?"

"How do I look?" she asked, smiling.

"Your color's high. Your eyes seem too bright," he said anxiously.

"I told you *why*. You're here."

"I'd like to take your temperature." He glanced around. He was a doctor again. Last night's fever could be persisting. "Where's the chart? Don't they have charts in this place?"

"Not when the nurse is supposed to be getting out of bed and going back to her room, Doctor."

"Jackson leave notes?" he asked sharply.

"He took them with him," she said complacently.

"I'll talk to Jackson. You know that."

"I know," she said. "But you worry too much. Are you sure you're not trying to get out of our date?"

He stared at her. *"Hell, no!"*

"Eight o'clock then," she said quickly. She looked at the door. "The house mother is coming back. She'll expect you to go now."

"Well .. ?" he said reluctantly. He listened. "Okay. Eight."

Behind him, he heard the house mother's heavy steps. The partially closed infirmary door opened.

"You're still here, Doctor?" she said.

"I was just leaving," he said. He looked down at Jane, his eyes going to the smooth column of her throat. She looked back at him steadily before he turned away. "I'll talk to Dr. Jackson. Good-bye. Rest as much as you can today."

The house mother walked to the door with him. "One of my best girls," she said confidentially. "Never any trouble. I'll send her back to her room and have someone change the bed. She's relieved of duty, so she can rest all day."

He nodded gravely, then glanced back. Jane Grant put her finger tips to her lips and blew him a kiss behind the house mother's back. He started to smile again.

Chapter Nine

The tables were empty, because it was early, and it was not one of the best restaurants. But looking around at the decorations and the spotless tablecloths with their gleaming cutlery laid out like the surgical instruments on a scrub nurse's wheeled stand, Jane Grant decided that she would always remember it.

Glen Carew's brown eyes watched her. As she returned his gaze, such a warm glow of feeling for him filled her that she had to look away. He looked younger, almost boyish tonight, and his soft charcoal-gray jacket, in such contrast to the hospital white coat, made him look even more handsome than she'd remembered.

When he smiled, she had seen laughter lines form at the corners of his steady eyes before she looked away.

"I was looking at the couple over in the corner," she said dreamily.

"Why?"

"She looks uneasy. What do you think he's saying to her?"

"Well, she's pretty," he said judiciously, looking that way now. "And she has nice legs. Maybe he's telling her that. But I'd take a bet on what he's thinking."

"What?"

"He's wondering when he can get her in the hay."

"Do all men think like that when they're out with a girl?"

He grinned. "I suppose, vaguely anyway, it's at the back of their minds. Surely your mother must have told you that?"

She smiled. "I don't remember her. My father divorced her when I was three. For a long time she was something that mustn't be discussed. Then he married again. Someone a lot younger than himself. About then, I decided that I wanted to be a nurse and live elsewhere."

"I'm sorry!" he said in quick contrition. He put his hand on hers where it lay on the table, and pressed it.

"It's nothing for you to be sorry about, Glen. For me perhaps. He died last year, and there was a time when I thought the world began and ended with him. And he seemed to think ... the same about me. But as I grew up, he changed. I think when he looked at me he saw my mother."

Glen Carew studied her in silence. "You were lonely?"

"Not after I became a nurse." The waiter was standing by their table. "I think I'd like a drink, Glen. A martini."

Carew ordered two and they were quickly set before them. It seemed strange suddenly that until now, he hadn't known anything about her really. He started telling her about himself. About a lake where he fished as a boy, how he'd almost drowned once.

She listened intently, seeing the word pictures he painted as clearly as if they were her own memories. And he was more accessible suddenly. It was as though they groped toward each other as they talked, finding one another for the first time.

"Nobody knows where we are," she thought. "Nobody cares. And we're together...."

"Another martini, before we order?"

The waiter hovered. He had brought the menu. It was long and varied, and most of it hand-written in French or Italian. Although it was not the best restaurant in Los Angeles, it had a name for good food. "I'd like another drink. Can we wait a bit longer?"

The waiter murmured assent and went away.

"Not hungry?" Carew smiled, his eyes a little anxious.

"No. But it isn't a symptom, Doctor. At least not of illness."

"Well," he said soberly. "I'm not hungry either. So maybe—? Well, I'll try not to worry about you."

"Something in the air," she said, smiling at him.

"Yes," he said, looking into her eyes.

"Glen, would you mind very much if we walked out of here?"

"Not if you want to." He looked around, seeing the garish decorations he hadn't noticed before. He said abruptly: "I don't know why I chose this damned place. Someone at the hospital mentioned it one day—"

"It isn't that, Glen. I like it!" she said quickly.

He tried to read her expression. He looked away. "It's just not for us tonight, eh? I feel that too."

"There were a lot of things I wanted to tell you last night, Glen," she said slowly. "I've still got them to say, and suddenly, it seems awfully urgent that I say them. Only ... not in a place like this."

"You're shivering," he said. "Are you cold?"

"It's a part of the way I feel," she said quietly. "As though time's standing still suddenly. Waiting for me. Like last night. When I waited for you to say things I wanted very badly to hear. At this moment I've a feeling that if I don't hurry, time will move on and I'll get left behind. So you see, everything has become urgent now and must be done quickly. Very quickly."

"Woman's intuition?" He was staring at her, puzzled. "What do you mean by everything?"

"I don't know! It's a little frightening."

"Very well." He stood up, came around behind her chair, and drew it back as she rose. "I've told you I'm in love with you," his lips said close to her hair. "That means that whatever you want to do, except make love with someone else, is okay with me."

"Thank you."

They walked toward the bar next to the entrance. The waiter waiting for their martinis looked up at them in surprise, and she watched Glen drop a bill on his tray. The surprise turned to a broad smile.

"Sorry we can't stay," Glen Carew said. "We thought of something else."

They walked down the steps, collars up against the bite of cold late November air that was bitter after the warmth of the restaurant.

THE DOCTOR'S PAST

Carew glanced around, and shook his head at a cruising cab, preparing to pull into the curb. "It's far too early for our show, Jane. Do you realize that?"

"You said whatever I wanted to do, that was all right with you. I don't want to go to a show, Glen."

"Okay," he said. "What?"

"Hold my arm tightly."

He did and she led him back toward where he had parked his car, a block away from the restaurant.

"Where are we going?" he asked.

"Somewhere out on the highway. I don't care where. I want to tell you the things I wanted to say last night." She didn't look at him. "I love you, Glen."

"I hoped that," he said. "It took you a long time to mention it."

His hand on her arm was drawing her off the sidewalk into the lighted entrance of a jeweler's shop. There were not many people on the sidewalks, although the night traffic was starting to move in steadily toward the center of the city. There was nobody in the shop except an elderly man with horn-rims, leaning on a showcase over a newspaper. He looked up expectantly as Glen Carew stopped her beside the lighted window.

Carew put his hands beneath her arms and drew her to him. His head bent and he kissed her.

She had never kissed anyone as she was kissing him, she realized. She seemed to be trying to make him a part of herself. His hands on her back held her against him so tightly that it hurt her breasts, but hurt was a part of pleasure. He drew away a little.

In the small silence as he looked at her, the man behind the showcase looked up over his glasses and then sauntered to the entrance. He opened the door and poked his head out dubiously. He might have been about to invite them in, or to protest their standing there like that.

Glen Carew turned toward the man and released her slowly. "It's okay," he said smiling. "We're getting married. We want to buy a ring."

"Oh," the man's face was cheerful suddenly. "I see!"

"Only I haven't asked her yet," Glen Carew said. He looked at Jane. "You will marry me, won't you, darling?"

She stared at him. "I thought—!"

"That I just wanted to neck with you?" he said. "I want to sleep with you, darling. All the nights...."

"I know...."

"I want you to have children. I'm not sure how many yet. But just as long as they look like you."

"Yes," she whispered.

"To the children, or the wedding?"

"To both," she said breathlessly.

"Then come on inside." His eyes were shining. "We're blocking the entrance to this good man's shop. He's a jeweler. He sells rings."

"I hadn't noticed till now," she said.

"Choose one." he said. "An engagement ring. We'll leave him a check and pick up the ring later. I don't carry that kind of money in bills. But pick a good one, the one you really want. Because I don't intend ever to let you go, so this may be the only engagement ring you'll ever have."

She looked at him slowly, her eyes dark. "I'll know the one I want."

They walked to the showcase hand in hand. The clerk beamed on them. He had already pressed the warning switch beneath his feet and another clerk had appeared behind a counter, where he could watch the customers while the first man bent for trays.

"Engagement and wedding rings—we have a very fine range," the elderly clerk said. "We try to make it a personal service at the House of Kramer. My name is Harrington. May I have your name, sir?"

"Carew. Dr. Glen Carew, I'm a resident at Midtown General Hospital," Carew told him. "Miss Grant is a nurse there. I'd like to leave a check for the ring and pick it up later, when the check is cleared at the bank. I'm afraid I only have about a hundred dollars with me in bills."

The clerk nodded. "We can arrange that, Doctor. Now what range are you interested in, Miss Grant?" He produced a tray of rings and displayed them. "This is what we call our thousand dollar range. You have beautiful hands, Miss Grant. Made for diamonds. Now in this setting at a thousand and fifty with two fine diamonds— But try it on. See it on your finger."

She shook her head. "I'd like to see something priced a lot less than that."

THE DOCTOR'S PAST

Carew smiled. "It's all right, Jane. Go higher if you wish. Just so long as it is the ring you want."

There was a twinkle in her eyes. "I can see the ring I want." She moved to the next showcase and bent, staring in. "Here it is," she said, pointing to one.

"But, Miss Grant," the clerk protested. "Those are very small diamonds. Some of them are . . . well, there are minute flaws. There's no comparison."

"How much?"

The clerk sniffed. "We call that our hundred dollar range. Now these—!"

"I'd like you to have something good, Jane," Carew ventured. "I was in the military hospital in the Orient for a long time, without much in the way of expenses."

"Whatever I want—remember?" she said slowly. "That's what you said. I don't want to wait until the check is cleared. I want it tonight, Glen. Now. And this one—it's exactly what I want."

"Diamonds are forever," the clerk protested. "Diamonds are an asset that never lose their value, Miss Grant."

"I'm sorry. I'll take this one. I have money with me in case Dr. Carew hasn't enough."

Carew nodded. "Very well. We'll take it." He added hearteningly, "Later perhaps she can choose another."

The clerk brightened. "Of course, Miss Grant. Take this ring for romantic reasons, tonight. It's one hundred and five dollars, including tax. Later I'll see what we can do about an exchange." He lowered his voice confidentially. "Bring the ring back to me and I'll see that you don't lose on it. It's a nice little ring. Will you try it on?"

"Please."

"Doctor, put it on her finger. They say that's lucky. That's it. That's fine! Comfortable? I'll put it in a gift box for you—"

"I'll wear it, thank you."

Carew counted the contents of his billfold and remembered the ten-dollar bill he kept in the back for emergencies. It left him five. He shook his head at her and she closed her bag again.

"Don't forget the name when you come back," the clerk said. "Arthur J. Harrington. It's on the card I gave you. Be sure to mention my name. I'll look after you. . . ."

It had grown colder outside, with the wind stinging their

faces as they walked into it. They walked close together holding hands, and now he could feel the ring with its small stone beneath his fingers.

"I love it," she said. "I'll never bring it back. I'll wear it forever."

"I thought every girl wanted a really good diamond engagement ring."

"I don't know what other girls want. Perhaps a lot of them just want an engagement ring. Any ring. I'm glad you stepped into that doorway, Glen." She laughed suddenly. "Just think—a few minutes ago we were just two people walking. Now we're an engaged couple."

He smiled. "Do you feel any different?"

"I can feel the ring. And a part of me that wasn't satisfied before, is satisfied now," she said quietly.

He drew her into the shelter of the parked car, while he unlocked the car door.

"Where are we going?" He helped her in, and slid into the driver's seat.

"Do you care?"

"Not if you're with me."

"North then."

"How far north?"

"When we get there, I'll know."

"The way it was with the ring?"

"Yes," she said. "Do you think I'm crazy tonight, Glen?"

"I love you," he said.

He drove steadily. The center of the city dropped behind, the highway took them through suburbs with white houses partially hidden by trees and gardens. A multi-lane highway opened up before them, curving northwest toward the sea, climbing steadily, with the city opening out behind them into a fairyland of colored lights.

"Look," she whispered. She spoke so close to his ear that it was as though her voice was his own thought. "There's an intersection up ahead. Could we turn off?"

"Why not?" he said. The big car steadied, slowed, then swung into the asphalt secondary road. He drove a few hundred yards. He parked. White rails showed on their right; below, they could see the lights of the city. A neon flashed somewhere close, trees masking it from where they'd stopped. "Here?" he asked.

"Yes!"

He switched off the lights, put his arms around her. "Now what did you want to tell me?"

"I love you," she said simply. "Last night there were so many things I wanted to say. It's funny! Now, I can't think of them. There's just that. That I love you, Glen."

"It's enough," he said.

She turned and let her body rest against him. He felt her tremble at the contact. His arms tightened. She stirred, only to move closer to him, to lean her face against his coat. She could feel his heart beating very hard against her cheek, but he did not move or speak for a long while. He just looked out at the sprawling city, holding her tightly.

"Where do we go from here, Jane?"

"We could see what the neon says."

"Would you like another drink? Something to eat?"

"No."

He felt her shiver suddenly within the circle of his arm. He tilted her face so that he could see her eyes.

"What's the matter, darling? You're trembling."

She gazed up at him. "I've fallen in love," she whispered. "And somehow I can't see past tonight. I'm frightened, and I just want to lock everything outside. I want you ... to love me, Glen."

"I'll take you back," he said hoarsely. "We can wait. We have a whole lifetime ahead of us." It wasn't going to be with Jane as it had been with Sue. That was past.

"Don't you want me, Glen? Now?" Jane's eyes were wide, and she was trembling.

"God!" he whispered, his face against her hair.

His fingers felt the ring on her finger. "I should have bought you a wedding ring. Tomorrow?"

"I don't want to think about tomorrow," she said softly. "I never liked that word."

He was kissing her then. Her lips, her throat. And she was responding to him, intensely aware of the touch of his hands, his lips.

"Jane, darling..." he murmured. "Jane..."

In that moment she wanted him frantically. She was ready to give herself completely, knowing only an unreasoned urgency. There seemed so little time....

But he was holding her away from him. "No, darling. No."

All her senses were on fire, her whole body seemed to be

burning. He held her firmly, his strength and control gradually stilling her desire.

"I'm sorry, Glen," she whispered. "I told you I was a little crazy tonight."

"Let's go back to the hospital," he said huskily. Seeing her look at him like that, he knew that if they stayed he could no longer be sure of himself. And he didn't want to hurt her. . . .

Chapter Ten

He came straight from the O.R., not waiting to change, striding anxiously down the long corridors in his short-sleeved white scrub suit.

"Good afternoon, Dr. Carew."

The passing nurse stared after him curiously. He neither heard nor saw her. He remembered only what her friend Diane Foster had said as she held a surgical glove pack for him in the annex.

"Jane said to tell you they've admitted her. She is over in one of the single rooms on the medical floor. She looks awful, Glen. They think it's a type of anemia."

"Who does?"

"Dr. Jackson. Dr. Baker from the clinic. They brought him up."

"Baker!" he'd said. "Baker?"

But Diane couldn't tell him any more than that. Anxiety was driving him desperately now to see Jane, blinding him to all else. Later, he'd talk to Jackson. See Baker if he was still in the hospital.

Anemia! There were any number of types of it, some less serious than others. There was no reason for him to be filled with dread, he told himself as he strode down the corridor. But Jackson had had her report from Pathology, and had called Baker in for consultation. This meant, perhaps, that they believed it to be really serious?

Yet—he kept telling himself as he walked—anemia was no longer a dread disease, not even when it was pernicious. You could learn to live with it. Like diabetes, science had almost mastered it.

The anemia would account for the syncope, the feverishness, and other things too. The way she had felt depressed, needing comfort, love, feeling a strange sense of urgency that had carried her into his arms that last night together. Like prescience. . . .

He walked past room twenty-five on the medical floor before he realized it. He turned abruptly and went back. With his hand upon the door he hesitated, realizing that the scrub suit, his anxiety, might not be reassuring—might seem to mean to her that he knew something that she did not.

"I'm not thinking like a doctor," he realized silently. "I'm thinking like a lover."

He knocked, then entered. A uniformed nurse bending over the bed straightened, showing momentary surprise before she smiled. He looked past the nurse to Jane. Her eyes warmed as she looked at him, but she was very pale. Her skin had the faint tint of jaundice, her young body beneath the frilly nightgown appeared fragile.

The nurse was reaching automatically for the chart. She said, "Dr. Baker and Dr. Jackson have just left, Doctor."

He looked at her. "This isn't a professional visit, Nurse."

The girl smiled and looked at Jane. "She's not supposed to have visitors. She even rates a special nurse. But of course, medical staff—that *is* different, isn't it?"

Jane said softly, "I just showed Miss Sawyer my ring."

"It's lovely," the nurse said, curious now as she looked at them both. Jane went on, "I was just about to tell you that Dr. Carew gave it to me, when he came in."

"You mean—?" The nurse's eyes widened.

"We're engaged to be married."

"Oh," the nurse said. "That's wonderful." She clipped the chart back on the stand.

"Wonderful," she said again in a low voice and turned away.

Carew stared at her profile, shocked. The nurse had been

THE DOCTOR'S PAST

close to tears. She had been very close to tears and he had seen pity in her eyes.

She gathered a cup and saucer from the locker near the bed and straightened without looking at him. "Does Dr. Jackson know that you're engaged?"

"You're the first one we've told," Jane said happily. "But I'm going to keep the ring on my finger now." She looked at Carew. "May I?"

"Of course," he said, smiling. "You had no right to take it off. And very soon, we're going to buy the wedding ring to go with it."

The nurse steadied the cup in its saucer. "I'm the *first* to know? I mean—"

She brushed past him, and he couldn't see her eyes again. She said quickly as she reached the door, "I'll just take these things away. I may be a...little while, Doctor...."

"Thank you," he said. "I'll stay until you get back."

He turned to Jane as the door closed. She was smiling up at him.

"I heard you coming along the passage. You walked past the door," she said accusingly. "Right past. Then you came back."

"You heard my footsteps?" he said, trying to smile.

"I've heard them before," she said. "In all sorts of places. A diet kitchen. In the operating room. In an alley one terrible night."

He sat on the edge of the bed. "I was so upset to hear you'd been admitted I walked right past.

"How do you feel, Janie?"

Her lips trembled and she couldn't answer him. For a long moment they looked at each other, then he was holding her suddenly, his face against hers.

"Darling," she whispered as she clung to him. "It's anemia, isn't it? I know the symptoms. I'm a nurse."

"If it is," he said, "that's nothing desperate. We'll build you up again. Baker's a wizard on blood disease. Maybe just a few weeks of bed rest, and therapy...."

He just held her then while they waited for the sounds of the special nurse's footsteps returning. And she cried so silently that he didn't know until he felt her tears against his cheek.

"I'm frightened, Glen," she whispered as she heard the footsteps coming. "Not for me—for us! I know what every nurse knows about anemia. That it can be checked. Often cured quickly. I know all that! But Glen, anemia is a symptom too... of other, far worse things."

Glen Carew sat on a chair in Dr. Jackson's office and looked around at the other three men dazedly. They looked back at him steadily, their three faces expressionless, their eyes narrowed slightly to veil pity.

"I'm sorry, Carew," Baker said quietly. "I didn't know you were interested in Miss Grant."

"Neither did I," Jackson said.

Prentice frowned from one man to the other. He looked at Baker. "You're sure?"

The specialist nodded. "I'm afraid there's no doubt. The pathological report is beyond dispute."

"I suspected anemia," Prentice said. He looked at Carew. "I reminded Dr. Carew that anemia was possible. But I thought...." He frowned again, and said quietly. "Therapy?"

"Jackson and I will commence therapy at once."

"It can't be!" Carew said through stiff lips. "No...."

"There's no doubt at all, Doctor," Baker said. "The diagnosis is positive. Miss Grant has leukemia. I'm sorry to have to tell you."

"With chronic leukemia they often live for years," Carew said defiantly. "It's possible. The blood count—"

"Thirty thousand leukocyte count, Doctor," Jackson said inexorably. He shook his head. "Don't delude yourself. It isn't chronic leukemia. *It's acute.* We can't change that. We can try to... slow it down. That's all."

Jackson said it gently, Carew knew. He was listening to a sentence of death for Jane. But his mind writhed away, would not accept it. It had to be chronic, not acute. It had to be something else, anything but acute leukemia that would surely kill her.... His mind shied abruptly away from the thought, took up the useless struggle again.

"Dr. Baker, you know more about it than any of us. There must be some mistake. You've seen her! Does she look like that? We went out together only the other night—" He choked, trying not to remember. Trying to think as a doctor fighting against disease, corruption, disintegration, death....

"Look at the facts, Doctor," Baker said coldly. "I'll run through them again for you. At first I hoped that she might have Jim Moreton's trouble, splenic anemia. The pathological report disproves that absolutely. The onset of acute leukemia is invariably abrupt as it was with her. It started with fever, and that has risen sharply now. It started with a tendency to hemorrhage. She's hemorrhaging now. Uterine hemorrhage. Not severe yet, but increasing slowly. She has severe and rapidly progressive anemia of the normocytic type, which presents a typical clinical picture of acute leukemia. Leukocyte count, as Jackson told you is right on thirty thousand. Hemoglobin is falling. Microscopic examination of the blood always—*and I mean always, Carew*—gives a correct diagnosis when it's carried out for a suspect acute leukemia."

"There's no enlargement of the spleen or the glands!" Carew protested desperately.

Baker nodded. "That's right. There isn't in her case. But I've seen many cases where there was no enlargement in the early stages, or even considerably later. They're often impalpable. Very often almost normal in appearance, until just before—before the disease terminates."

Carew looked up, his dark eyes moist. He bit his bottom lip.

Baker shook his head, and looked away. "I'm sorry, Dr. Carew...."

"Therapy!" Carew said. "You mentioned therapy. We can't just . . . do nothing!"

"We'll try everything we know," Jackson said, trying to keep sympathy from his voice. "We're doctors, Carew."

Prentice cleared his throat. "How about the use of ACTH? Cortisone? Some remissions have been obtained, isn't that true?"

"Very brief," Jackson said.

"Some people are experimenting with drugs intended to interfere with the division of the leukemic cells and so stop their multiplying," Baker said. He shrugged. "Nothing positive there yet, although mercaptopurine seems the most promising so far. There have been some remissions with it. And there's methotextrate. And nitrogen mustard has been sometimes helpful. We'll try everything we can, Doctor. I intend to contact a friend in the East tonight. He's been carrying out some of the experiments. If there's anything that seems to have a chance, we'll try it."

He looked at Baker, but couldn't feel gratitude. "Transfusions! Damn it, transfusions must help. Normal blood...."

He still felt dazed. He could neither understand fully what was happening yet, nor think as a doctor.

Prentice said, "We can't overload the circulation, Dr. Carew. You know that."

He knew it. But he said stubbornly, "Baker said she was hemorrhaging already. We can replace that lost blood."

Prentice looked at Baker, who nodded, frowning. "We will as soon as that's possible. I'll run a blood volume test. But Carew, we have to remember...."

He felt that they were alien suddenly. They were trying to prove that it was impossible for Jane to live. He couldn't accept that.

"We'll transfuse her with packed red cells!" he cried. "And don't tell me that's not possible. In reconstructive surgery, I've used the concentrated packed red-cell transfusions where there was a developing anemia from earlier hemorrhage. It doesn't overload the circulation. It must restore the balance—"

He stared around at them defiantly, angrily. Baker was frowning at the open window and the hospital grounds below. The wind that came into the room suddenly touched Carew's face with cold fingers. Prentice got up and closed the window.

The service chief came back and said quietly, "I've used packed red-cell transfusions also, Doctor. Couldn't it help?"

"It might," Baker said slowly. "It might. But, it could cause clotting. It does that sometimes, and proves fatal. Even in the anemias. But—it sounds reasonable. I haven't seen it used for leukemia."

"It's more viscid," Prentice said, frowning. "You'd have to give it very slowly."

"It could add the deficient factor to the blood stream," Jackson said.

They looked at one another.

Baker nodded. "All right. We'll try a packed red-cell transfusion, as Dr. Carew suggests." He stood up and looked at his watch. "When you're ready, Jackson, I think we'll see her again. We'll give her five hundred cc.s and see what happens. We might even see a remission. It's possible."

"She could be given more as the hemorrhage continues," Prentice said. "Perhaps further remissions?"

Baker shook his head. He looked at Carew steadily. "There's one thing we all know about the acute leukemias.

They're rapidly and inevitably fatal. Nothing we do can alter that. We can't keep on replacing all the blood in her veins with normal blood. We can't keep the balance that way. And even if by some God-given chance we could, there would still be other deterioration going on. In the tissues. The organs. Bone marrow. Her body is no longer able to keep the balance of metabolism. Leukemia is not a disease of blood loss, but of the production of abnormal blood cells. Nothing can save her life." He was vehement suddenly. "You have to make your mind up about that, Dr. Carew. You have to accept it."

"No!" Carew put his head in his hands. A low groan broke from him. "No...."

Prentice said in a low voice, "She has no relatives? Nobody else to tell?"

"A stepmother somewhere in the East. She doesn't know where. No. There's nobody, and no estate involved."

"Has Miss Grant been told?"

"Just that she has a progressive anemia," Baker said. He shrugged. "But I think she knows it's worse. Very often the patient knows. Have you found that?"

"You can't tell her?" Prentice asked.

"No. Could you?"

"Hell!" Prentice said in a harsh voice. "That young girl—!"

He heard their voices through his hands. Baker's hand gripped his shoulder briefly. Then Jackson's. They were going, silently. He forced himself to look up, bewildered.

"I'm sorry! But it just came out of the blue. Yesterday...." Carew couldn't go on. He could only look at them, Baker and Jackson standing near the door, looking back at him— Prentice staring angrily out the window at the bleak buildings that were being whipped by the cold wind heralding in December.

"December..." he thought. "Oh God!"

He said, quietly now, "How long, Doctor?"

Baker moved uneasily. "You're a doctor. You know as well as I that you can't say exactly. You can never be sure of anything, except that a disease is terminal. Fatal. It runs its course slowly, or it ends quickly. You can generalize—say, in some cases with acute leukemia, a few months. Or—"

"How long, Dr. Baker?" Carew insisted.

"Goddammit!" Baker said violently. *"What do you want*

from me? No matter what we do, she won't live through the coming year."

Carew watched numbly as Baker walked out and closed the door. The words seemed to be torn from Carew: "I won't accept it!"

He became aware of Prentice standing near him and looked up.

"I can't accept it, Doctor!"

"Baker will win her remissions," Prentice said gently. "He's a good man. She'll have periods of time when she may even feel quite well after therapy. And she doesn't really *know*. Have you thought about that?"

Carew shook his head.

"People sometimes sense death when it's not far off," Prentice said slowly. "But they never really accept it as coming to them. To anyone else—but never to themselves. Not until they're *in extremis,* and then at last quiet acceptance comes. You've seen that over and over again. Up to the last, they hope, they have their moments of happiness."

"Do you think that makes it any easier?"

"Give her as many of those moments as you can, Glen. Let her hope and dream, if you really love her. In our profession we're taught to mask personal thought, personal feeling. Don't let her *see* what you're feeling. If you do and she loves you, you'll destroy her. *Don't let her know!* And when it comes, it will come easily, gently.... Maybe she'll still dream on? Who knows?"

"What about me?" he said in agony. "I love her—"

"You're a surgeon. Other people's lives depend on your ability to keep on. Help them, and you'll be helping yourself. You'll find the hurt will lessen as you work—now, and later."

"I couldn't do that to her!" he cried. "It would be too cruel ... too cruel! Oh God...."

"Well, well, well " Dr. Baker said heartily. "Color in your cheeks this morning. What do you think, Doctor? Is she looking better?"

"She always looks like a million to me," Glen Carew said.

"Another remission, eh?" Baker said. "And this time we can't be sure whether it was my drug or Dr. Carew's concentrated red-cell transfusion last night—can we?"

THE DOCTOR'S PAST

"I'll give you half credit each," Jane Grant said, trying to smile. She moved weakly against the pillows, favoring her left arm, still painful from last night's transfusion.

Carew moved back from where he had been sitting when Baker walked in. He watched the burly specialist take the chart and study it briefly through his bifocals. Baker grunted noncommittally.

"Fever down a little too, eh?"

"One of the best mornings she's had since we admitted her," Carew said cheerfully. "The transfusion, of course."

"Surgeons!" Baker said. He winked at Jane. "Never satisfied unless they're cutting holes in people to put blood in or take it out. I'm going to prod you a little this morning, Jane. Hope you don't mind?"

"Would it make any difference if I did?"

He began his examination and Carew stepped back. He walked to the window and looked out, after that first glance. He hadn't noticed it before, but she was losing weight rapidly. Her small breasts seemed shrinking and as Baker palpated the upper abdomen, he had seen her ribs plainly as palpation tightened the chest wall's superficial tissues.

Her face was thinning also, so that now she seemed to have high cheekbones, giving her an almost Slav appearance. But her eyes were wide and bright each time he entered the room. They still held the warm glow that he saw at nights when he tried to sleep.

He turned back. Jane was watching him as Baker gestured to adjust the covers again. He smiled.

"There's quite a lot of sly work going on in the wards," he said. "You can't open a cupboard without seeing Christmas decorations. I just saw your friend Diane coming over from the nurses' home with a big cardboard box."

"Yes," she said. "I know. For the patients. It's almost Christmas."

"You can feel it in the air," Baker said. "Well, as a special concession, Jane, I'm going to let you eat Christmas dinner tomorrow."

"Are you releasing me from my diet?" she asked eagerly. "Does that mean I'm really improving?"

"You've improved this morning," Baker said. "You've even a little color. Last night you were yellow as a lemon."

"*I was not!*" she said indignantly.

"Well, maybe only a very light lemon," Baker said, grinning. "So tomorrow—Christmas dinner."

"Transfusion again tonight?" Carew asked.

"I'll think about it. The hemorrhage seems to have lessened. Perhaps not. I'll look in again this afternoon and decide." He looked around for the nurse. "Oh, Miss Curtis—will you come to my office?"

"Yes, Doctor."

"Dr. Carew, I'd like to speak to you for a moment?"

Jane looked at Carew wistfully. "Will I see you this afternoon?"

"This afternoon? I'll see you again in—" He looked at Baker. "How long, Doctor?"

"Five minutes," Baker said, smiling. "Don't you have any surgery this morning, Doctor?"

"Everyone seems to be avoiding surgery till after Christmas," Carew said. "The schedule doesn't start today until eleven."

"I don't blame 'em!" Baker said. "I'll see you this afternoon again, my dear. Keep that color, won't you?"

"I'll try," she said. They went out and she pursed her lips at Glen Carew as he closed the door.

Carew looked at the other man anxiously as he followed him a few yards along the corridor.

Baker smiled at the nurse. "See if you can find me a cup of coffee, Nurse. I had calls all night, and I can use one. Bring a cup for yourself down to the clinic. Dr. Carew will stay with her for a while."

"Yes, Doctor." The nurse smiled at him understandingly and walked back toward the diet kitchen.

"Another remission," Carew said tentatively. "She's bright. Her color is better. The fever is down a few points."

"Symptomatic relief," Baker said, frowning. "I'm afraid I've bad news, Glen."

Carew looked at him wearily, unsmiling. "The spleen?"

"You noticed, eh? Yes. It's swelling. Arsenic therapy reduced it for a while, and lowered the fever. Now that's losing therapeutic value." He shrugged. "I could try deep ray, but I doubt that she could stand it. It reduces the spleen. We're going to have to discontinue the mercaptopurine. It's too nauseating, and she's reached the highest dosage we can give her. That only leaves one of the nitrogen mustard derivatives."

THE DOCTOR'S PAST

Carew sighed. "By injection?"

"Yes. Notice her veins? Injections by the IV route are becoming difficult."

"I'll give them."

"Very well." Baker looked along the corridor into the ward at its end. "Christmas! Sometimes it's depressing. There's one remarkable thing about Jane Grant. Her cheerfulness. She seems almost happy. Well, you two are in love, and you're around. . . ."

"I spend every moment I can get with her," Carew said.

"And you talk. Dream a little, as though nothing bad could ever happen, eh? Yes, she's told me. Well—it's helped her."

"It's helped us both," Carew said.

"Yes. . . ." Baker stood silently for a moment. He cursed. "Hell, Carew—I hate to tell you this. I got the latest path. report this morning. We've held the total leukocyte count on thirty thousand for three weeks or more. And now, suddenly, it's shot way up. It's almost a hundred thousand."

Carew stared at him in consternation. "Then the nitrogen mustard—?"

"I wish I knew," Baker sighed. "But I don't. We can only hope that it will give another remission, and try it."

"If it doesn't?"

Baker frowned. "Deep ray therapy."

"But you said—?" He broke off, appalled, seeing the clinical picture. Seeing the last resort tried and failing. He found control. "You've done everything possible. Thank you, Doctor. I'll go back now."

Baker nodded. "Don't let her see—" His eyes held those of the younger man. "You wouldn't, of course! Sometimes I wish . . ." His voice trailed. "Stay with it, Glen."

He went off down the passage heavily.

A nurse walked past, but Glen Carew did not see her. He turned back slowly, remembering that Jane would be listening for his footsteps. He walked more briskly.

She smiled at him as he came in.

"A man of his word!" she said.

"Five minutes on the dot!" He could feel his lips trembling. He fought for control. "Do you feel like talking, Jane?" he said and sat on the edge of the bed.

"I always do when it's with you, darling."

"You say the nicest things," he said. It had become a

game with them, the way they talked together now when they were alone. And sometimes he thought that she knew the things they said were only play words. That they could never have reality.

But they played it just the same.

"Have you been out today, darling?"

"I went downtown to buy you a Christmas present," he said. "As soon as the stores opened. Only I'm not going to tell you what it is until tomorrow."

"Can I guess?"

"No," he said. "You're too good at guessing."

"I got Diane to get me something for *you*, so I won't tell you what it is either! It's in the locker. Diane helped me giftwrap it. I always liked Christmas shopping. Were the stores crowded?"

"It was early," he said.

"I wish I could have gone with you."

"You will," he said. "Next Christmas."

"We'll be married then."

"Long before then."

He put his arms around her so that she couldn't see his face. He held her like that, gently, waiting for the nurse to come back, lowering her back onto her pillows when he heard the tap of the nurse's footsteps outside.

"Good-bye, darling," she whispered. "See you again soon."

"This afternoon, Janie," he promised. He adjusted the mask. He smiled at the nurse. He walked outside...

Throughout his eleven o'clock operation, he thought about her. He was finding now that he could think of her with a part of his mind that seemed apart. There was relief in work. He looked in at noon, and she was not as well. The remission was passing. The faint tinge of jaundice was coming back. She was weaker, drowsy, barely able to talk to him.

He started the nitrogen mustard therapy, joking with her about it—telling her that she would not have to take the oral drug any more now because she looked so well.

In the dining room he tried not to see the sympathy in the eyes of his colleagues. He did not eat.

On the way back to see her again, he heard Jackson's name being paged over the P.A. system. Suddenly he was running, his heart sick.

Jackson was there. He had raised the foot of the bed, was

THE DOCTOR'S PAST

reviving her with oxygen. He frowned as Carew came in, warning him to go away, but Jane had already seen him. Her sick eyes tried to focus on him, but he bent quickly to soothe her.

"Glen ... Glen?" she whispered weakly.

"I'm here, darling."

"Not ... so good ..." she whispered. "We need another ... remission, don't we, darling?"

"We'll organize one," he promised. He straightened and looked at Jackson.

"The nitrogen mustard isn't having any effect," Jackson said. "I'll call Baker. We'll have to change it."

"Back to one of the others?"

"Radiation therapy."

"No," he said. "Transfusion. Concentrated red-cell."

Jackson shook his head. Jane's drowsy eyes had closed again. He bent to examine the pupils and straightened. "She's in coma again."

Carew looked at the nurse. "Transfusion set, Nurse. Concentrated red-cell suspension. *Stat!*"

She nodded and ran.

"Baker's doubtful about the concentration," Jackson said, frowning.

"It worked before. Deep ray won't. We all know that."

"Not till we try—we don't," Jackson said.

Carew frowned. "All right. Call Baker. I'll go on with the transfusion."

"Check her B.P. and pulse," Jackson said. "I'll be back."

When the nurse hurried in, he had her arm strapped to the armrest, the standard for the transfusion in place. He worked fast, preparing the area, pinching the flaccid vein that seemed even more difficult to find. The needle slid in, and he started the flow of concentrated red cells. The viscid blood dripped slowly, thirty drops to the minute. He bent anxiously, checking pulse and pressure, almost holding his breath as the slow seconds ticked away. Each two seconds, a drop fell, entered the vein, was absorbed, passed into the diseased blood stream, strengthening it ... adding red cells....

"Thank God!" he whispered.

There was improvement suddenly. She moved her right hand weakly. The sphygmomanometer started to register pressure that was a little higher. The pulse felt stronger.

And miraculously then, as they both watched, Jane opened her eyes slowly. Her lips twitched in a smile as she saw him.

He sat down on the chair, hearing Jackson's rapid footsteps as he came back. He saw that the nurse was crying.

Jackson bent quickly over Jane.

"What did Dr. Baker say?" Carew asked.

"He's coming over," Jackson replied. "Ten minutes. He's going to start deep ray. At once."

"What did he say about the transfusion?"

Jackson's shrug was weary. "If you want it; it's your risk. It makes no difference."

"It makes a lot of difference," Carew said. "She's conscious again already. I'm due in the O.R. I'll come back in an hour."

"We'll both be here," Jackson said.

He kissed Jane and went out.

He scrubbed. He went through the cleansing ritual. He picked up the scalpel. He made the first incision. He had never found Linton as clumsy as an assistant. Or Wilson as unsure. But his own fingers seemed to have taken on an intelligence of their own. He had never worked as smoothly.

And the part of his mind that was not seeing Jane, knew that Prentice was right. Surgery, work was the answer. There would always be work. Always be someone needing his skill.

The operation ended. He called the medical floor. Jane was conscious and talking to the nurse. Baker had decided to give the first radiation treatment later in the day. She was responding to the transfusion.

He went back to the next patient, already waiting in the operating room. It was an appendectomy and he finished it in fourteen minutes. He could go back to her now. He washed up fast, and slipped into his coat. He hurried to the elevators and down to the medical floor. Prentice was coming slowly out the door of twenty-five.

The service chief's eyes were dull in an expressionless face. Carew stopped abruptly.

"Five minutes ago," Prentice said gently. "There wasn't time to send for you. She's dead, Glen."

"*No!*" he cried.

"She'd just talked to the nurse about you. She asked for a

THE DOCTOR'S PAST

comb and began to tidy her hair. She said you'd be along soon. She felt nothing. She just lay back, waiting for you. The nurse noticed that her eyes were open. Baker's in there."

"She was having another remission," he said thickly. "She can't be... dead...."

"I'm sorry, Glen," Prentice said. "It was a clot. We're sure of it. An occlusion."

"Oh, no!" he said. "No!"

He had turned abruptly and was walking away, not even aware that he was walking.

Prentice's voice came after him faintly: "Glen, wait...."

Carew took no notice.

There was no elevator at the floor. He went down the stairs, past the reception desks and clinics, and out through the hospital gates. He was aware only of a great numbness. A sense of loss that was immeasurable, infinite....

If he stopped walking, he felt that he would sink down wherever he happened to be. He walked on....

He lost all sense of time and place. Afterward he would remember the Christmas shoppers who stepped aside to let him pass; the decorated windows. He walked a long way from the hospital, into an area of the city that he did not know.

The first sensation he had was of leaning with his face on his arm against a brick wall. He was very cold. And he was still in his hospital coat. He was shivering.

But he was not alone.

Dr. Stanley Prentice was standing beside him. The wall he was leaning against belonged to a tenement that bore a demolition notice.

He looked at Prentice dazedly. "How did you get here?"

"I followed you, Glen. I have a car around the corner. I'll take you back."

"Baker was right about the danger of clotting, wasn't he? I... gave her the transfusion, and...."

"I choose to think you gave her a few more hours of life. So does Dr. Baker. He told Jackson that it was a calculated risk. He said he agreed with the transfusion. It revived her temporarily. Nothing could have done more than that. Nothing."

"I think I'd like to see her," he said.

"I'll drive you back...."

Glen Carew climbed the steps, smiled automatically at the stewardess, and sank into the seat of the plane. Through the window beside him he could see the city, the bulk of Los Angeles Midtown Hospital low down among the tall buildings on the horizon.

A lot of memories lay there, and for a little while they'd lived again, as he walked from place to place and remembered. Now, waiting for the other passengers to settle in their seats, he thought of the long months that had followed Jane's death. Prentice had been right about a lot of things, it's true, but it had been months before he was proved right about the relief that work could provide. Carew had gone to pieces after her death. This was something he had been trying not to remember, putting the recollection of it away from him, almost as if it belonged to someone else. Now he could squarely face the memory of it—the weeks when he sat inert, unfeeling, unthinking in a hospital room, wishing only to be dead himself... the gradual recovery, the regressions which came less and less frequently... the return, finally, to life and work.

And it had been work that had completed his healing, lessened his pain. It did not matter that now, at this moment, this whole period of his life had become so vivid again. That also would pass. Hurt lessened with time, and there was always work. Prentice had said that.

He watched the panel flash and fastened his belt.

Jane had been warm and sincere, she had loved him. There had been moments as he visited old places when memories revived, when she had seemed very close to him again.

She would not want him always to be lonely.

Or unhappy.

The lights were coming on in the city, the fading remnants of sunset touching ragged clouds in the west with a grandeur of gold and red. The plane lifted smoothly, with the city falling behind, sprinkled with lights that were rapidly becoming meaningless with distance. Only the tints in the sky remained—a golden sheen, like a woman's hair, but changing subtly, becoming red....

It reminded him of more recent memories. Of another nurse who loved him, a red-haired girl with steady gray eyes.

Glen Carew smiled as he looked out the window of the

THE DOCTOR'S PAST

speeding plane at the sunset. As yet, those old memories seemed too close. Too vivid. He had turned a knife in an old wound, and for a while the pain would be renewed.

But perhaps, one day....

Other SIGNET Nurse and Doctor Fiction

EMERGENCY NURSE   **by Jane Converse**
> A plastic surgeon fights to save a boy's life, a girl's future, and his own shattered romance. (#S2079—35¢)

NIGHT WARD   **by Noah Gordon**
> A pretty nurse must choose between a socially prominent surgeon and a young policeman. (#S2114—35¢)

NOT AS A STRANGER   **by Morton Thompson**
> One of the most widely read novels of our time, this powerful story of a dedicated doctor established new records as a bestseller. (#Q2209—95¢)

THE CRY AND THE COVENANT   **by Morton Thompson**
> The world-famous medical novel about the heroic doctor who gave his life to save mothers and their newborn children. (#T1819—75¢)

SCALPEL (abridged)   **by Horace McCoy**
> An absorbing novel about a coal miner's son who becomes a successful society surgeon, and the two women who help him discover his true destiny. (#P2235—60¢)

ALOHA NURSE   **by Ethel Hamill**
> The explosive romance between a nurse devoted to her career at a hospital in Hawaii and a talented doctor dedicated to the pursuit of money. (#S2022—35¢)

LIMBO TOWER   **by William Lindsay Gresham**
> In the TB ward of a hospital, a man facing death draws strength from a nurse, while helping her overcome fears that have thwarted her life. (#D2046—50¢)

TO OUR READERS: If your dealer does not have the SIGNET and MENTOR books you want, you may order them by mail, enclosing the list price plus 5¢ a copy to cover mailing. If you would like our free catalog, please request it by postcard. The New American Library of World Literature, Inc., P. O. Box 2310, Grand Central Station, New York 17, New York.